TWO
COMPLETE WESTERN NOVELS.
A $4.50 value for only $2.25

NELSON
NYE

GUN FEUD AT TIEDOWN
AND
ROGUE'S RENDEZVOUS

Other ACE Books by Nelson Nye:

GUN FEUD AT TIEDOWN

NELSON NYE

ace books
A Division of Charter Communications Inc.
A GROSSET & DUNLAP COMPANY
51 Madison Avenue
New York, New York 10010

GUN FEUD AT TIEDOWN
Copyright © 1965 by Nelson Nye

An ACE Book

Published simultaneously in Canada

2 4 6 8 0 9 7 5 3 1
Manufactured in the United States of America

I

Looking back you might be inclined to think most of the trouble had likely broken loose about the time the cow crowd—crocked to the gills that Saturday night, and more for the hell of it than anything else—proposed "Butterfly" Jones for high sheriff of Tiedown.

And you'd have been half right. The gamblers and chippies had gone along with the gag and the country's toughs had voted him in. There'd been a heap of backslapping and considerable relief when the erstwhile law, sans shine of tin, had disappeared inside the southbound coach, which had promptly taken off like hell wouldn't have it.

The sleepy old town shook itself awake and took "a new lease on life," as they say in the papers. Money began to jingle and flow, new blood came in—the boom was on in feverish earnest, with street frontages selling at undreamed of prices and everyone flushed with this new excitement. It was a matter of indifference that two stages were stopped, Gattison's Print Shop wrecked, the Weekly Beller suspended. A ripple of talk made its rounds of the cow camps when the Purple Cow honky-tonk was taken for its cash at the point of a gun by three masked bandits.

But it wasn't until Harley Ferguson was found with pockets pulled out and his head caved in behind Bernagrowt's saddle shop some three weeks later, that a group of the town's more sober-minded citizens descended in a body on that prince of good fellows, the astonished Price Jones.

He'd been snoring it off in his grubby-looking underwear on the Army-surplus cot he'd moved into his office, a half-emptied bottle on the floor at his side. Disheveled and baffled, he sat up in his drawers to peer, bleary-eyed, at the indignant town fathers. "Wh—whasha matter?"

"Matter! Now see here," T. Ed Gretchen, the town's banker, said toothily, "you're holding this job under sufferance, you know!" And Eph Wilson, proprietor of Tiedown's largest mercantile store, declared with the look of a censorious beetle: "Either you straighten up quick and get down to business—the business you're drawing your stipend for—or you'll turn over that badge to someone that kin!" And the rest of them nodded with self-righteous scowls.

Jones, with his jaw dropped open, blinked up at them stupidly. He fumbled a hand across unshaven cheeks and levered his ungainly length off the cot to stagger erect with an unstifled belch. "Whashat?"

It was hot in the office. The banker said, grimacing: "The man's impossible!" and patted his moist cheeks with a bit of crumpled linen. Growls rose from the others, and Flancher—who kept the town's only hotel—shook an irate finger under the new sheriff's nose. "By Gawd, Jones, we demand protection! You wanta go back to punchin' cows for a livin'?"

Jones grabbed up a bucket and reeled out to the pump. By the sounds of it, it hadn't been greased since Noah. He came back, still spluttering and dripping. With that scrawny mustache he looked more than ever like an underfed gopher, but at least he could move without stumbling into things.

His nose was too long, coming down like a beak over that ten-haired top lip. He made a gangling, slat-thin, shuffling shape, long-necked, bowlegged, oddly hunched through the shoulders as though the weight of that outsized lump in his neck was just about all that a fellow could tote. As a cow nurse Jones had made a pretty fair hand, but cows weren't everything—even around here—and Flancher, eyeing him, was too disturbed to care a hang about tact. "You're a helluva lookin' specimen!"

The sheriff pawed sheepishly at his rumple of hair. "Guess," he said, "I must've tied on a beaut."

"What've you done about them stickups?"

"I'm workin' on them."

3

Five pairs of eyes stared back without favor. "If practice makes perfect," Bernagrowt began grumpily—but the hotel man cut in. "You got any idear what's been happening round here?"

Jones, peering about uneasily, mumbled: "Don't reckon you gents'd be so riled over nothin'."

"Nothing!" T. Ed Gretchen dragged his wilted handkerchief distractedly over his face again. "You're about as feeble an excuse for a peace officer as it's been my misfortune ever to come up against."

"An' we ain't goin' to stand fer it!" Bernagrowt tucked in, flapping his arms like a goonie stretching.

"Gentlemen—please!" Jones gulped with both hands to his head. "If somebody'll tell me—"

"You hear about that card game in the Aces Up last night?"

Jones, with extreme caution, shook his head.

Wilson growled, "That minin' fella, Ferguson, come out high man. When the game broke up he had his pockets stuffed full—"

"An' turned up this mornin' with his head bashed in," Bernagrowt finished, "out back of my shop!"

"We want to know," the banker added, "what you propose to do about it. And your tenure in office as sheriff of this county will be determined—you might as well know this—by the results of your inquiry into Ferguson's brutal end!"

Having said this, T. Ed Gretchen put his handkerchief away, and, flanked by his satellites, irascibly departed.

Jones, groaning piteously, sagged to his cot and took his pounding head in both miserable hands. It was plain he was going to have to pull himself together, at least make a show of looking into that killing; but this wasn't a matter he felt up to tackling with his head whirling round like a chip in a millrace.

He floundered up, still groaning, and stomped into his boots. He got his hat, a cream-colored Stetson of the twelve-gallon variety, with a brim broad enough to keep the rain off his face—if any ever got to showing up in this country, where the oldest frog hadn't learned how to swim.

He stood there, frowning, with his mind on the drought and the cost of keeping horses in a desert where caterpillars and termites got the lion's share of what little grass infrequently came up. Then, his thoughts jumbling round again to Ferguson's misfortune, he fumbled into a blue-silk, go-to-hell shirt with red roses appliqued across the shoulders, and reached for the fawn-colored charro pants he'd got out of last night after caterwauling home from the Florencias' fandango. Glaring at the pants, he flung them down in disgust.

He'd thrown out all his work clothes when he'd quit his job at Rafter, not figuring to have any more use for them in the soft berth of sheriff in a place like Tiedown, whose greatest excitement in the past two terms had been the shrieks of the

Widow Henry the time that horned toad had got into her bed.

Jones scowled longingly at his own. For two cents, by grab, he would've pounded his ear until his head felt more like tying into this business. He stood considering it seriously for a moment, then, with a shuddering sigh, he hauled his second-best pants from the tangled plunder wadded up in his warsack, and hopped around on one boot trying to pull the things on.

He was still clumsily trying, through a flow of abusive language, when a blocky, powerful bear of a man came shoving his forceful way through the door.

The guy came to a stand-still in scuffed, batwing chaps, pushing back the hat from his face the better to observe the sheriff's predicament. "Damn if you ain't a sight for sore eyes!" the big walloper said, cocking his head from one side to another. "Where the hell'd you dig up pants like them? Godey's Ladybook?"

Jones flushed with resentment. This was catalogue stuff he'd sent clean to Fort Worth for— the yellow boots alone had set him back two months' pay! "WHAT THE WELL-DRESSED CATTLEMAN WILL BE WEARING THIS FALL," was the heading on the page from which he'd made his selection. Let the dumb bastard laugh, he thought with disdain, and sank into a chair, thrusting out his bowlegs. "Catch hold of them boots, will you?"

Long Creek Trimbo wasn't pulling off boots for

nobody. Looking down at Jones scornfully he blew out his cheeks. Planting both rope-scarred hands on his hips he began to swell up like a mule in a hailstorm, but the look of Jones was too much for him and he let his breath go in a snort of laughter. "The Great Seizer!" he hooted, then said derisively: "When you goin' to git onto yourself?"

Jones glowered, downright humiliated, putting on such a show before a dumb ox like Trimbo. He got the other boot into that dangling leg, and, though he dang near popped the seam in his anger, forced the stubborn boot through, and hauled the seat of the pants up over his butt. Fastening the front of them he caught up his shell belt, flung it about him, cinching it angrily. "This a slack stretch at your place?"

The man from Quarter Circle S took a hard, tighter look at him. "Waste of time, I reckon—told Geetch as much, but he was bound an' determined—"

"If this palaver's got a point how about short-cuttin' to it?"

Spangler's range boss said: "We had a horse hooked last night."

Jones, blinking, stared. "You pullin' my leg?"

"Any time I ride a dozen miles two ways through this kinda heat you better believe it ain't fer no joke. The horse was stolen. Geetch wants him back."

Price Jones looked like he didn't know yet if he was minded to swallow it. He'd heard some mighty mean things about Long Creek Trimbo and suspected that mostly they'd been told with restraint. Folks generally figured to give him plenty of room. Trimbo, maybe, didn't go out of his way to find a use for his talent, but the word had got around and no one who had sampled it wanted a second helping.

So now Jones said, as though feeling his way, "I ain't doubtin' your word, but you got to admit it don't sound a heap likely."

Trimbo grunted. "Crazier'n popcorn on a hot stove. If it had been Eight Below or Curtain Raiser even, a man might figure to make some sense of it. But the one that's gone is Papago Pete, a stove-up ol' geldin' no guy in his right mind would give fifty cents fer."

Jones scrubbed a hand across red-rimmed eyes. "Maybe he just sort of wandered off."

"Didn't happen that way." Trimbo shook his head, scowling. "Some joker come right on into the yard, let down a couple bars an' cool as you please, put a hackamore on him, led him out to the road, hopped aboard an' took off."

Jones stared blankly. He couldn't see that it even began to make sense. And it made even less sense that a case-hardened bunch like Quarter Circle S would fetch a piddlin' deal like this to the law, when all of the years for as long as Price Jones had known anything about them, Spangler's outfit had run roughshod over anything and anyone that got in its way. Them and Grisswell's Gourd & Vine had just about, between them, run this country.

"The old man sick?"

"Geetch? Hell, no."

"So why come to me?"

"What I ast him myself, an' you know what he said?"

Jones shook his head.

"Said he didn't want to embarrass you. Said you was new to the job an' the least we could do was give you a chance to prove the voters hadn't made no mistake."

Jones peered suspiciously. "He never brought nothin' to the law before."

"My very words," Trimbo nodded, cuffing the dust from his hat. "He explained that, too. Said times was changin' an' if it didn't discommode him he was willin' to change with 'em." The range boss grinned. "Get your nag an' let's go."

"Don't rush me," Jones flared. "Got all I can do right here for this morning. We had a killin' last night—"

"Could have another," Trimbo said mighty quiet, "if you an' me ain't arrived by the time Geetch gits there."

II

Dust devils danced and the heat bore down as
the sun climbed higher in a glare of sky and the
wilted morning limped toward noon. Even the liz-
ards had dug in out of sight, and the groaning
Jones on the rack of his hangover bitterly wished
he were dead a dozen times before they had been
an hour on the road.

Heat lay over everything like a wriggling film,
and off in the distance blue mountains shimmered
as though shaped out of gelatin and tossed down
still quivering. The sheriff closed burning eyes. His
head felt tighter than a pounding drum but at least
his stomach had finally quit churning, though he'd
have felt a heap better if he could have downed his
breakfast coffee. While saddling his horse he tried
to pry a few facts out of Trimbo, but this had been
about as helpful as hectoring a gatepost.

The country's vast silence began to get on his nerves. He still couldn't figure how he had got to be sheriff, but the badge on his shirt had opened a heap of doors he hadn't previously noticed, and in this new, enlarged view, the life he had come from had lost all its savor. Never had it looked so unpalatably bleak as it did right now, thinking back to that powwow he had just come away from. Them merchants was sure enough on the peck, and T. Ed Gretchen, besides being banker, was chief county commissioner—not the kind for talking just to hear his noggin rattle. He meant every dadgummed word of it!

Jones pried open his eyes to slant a covert look at Trimbo. The tough, beefy shine of that slab of a face did not encourage questions, but the banker's ultimatum finally drove Jones into voice.

"I want to know where you're takin' me."

Spangler's range boss, grunting, did not even look around.

Jones did not want any trouble with Trimbo but as sheriff he felt he deserved more than that. Grunts were for pigs and after stewing a while in squirming frustration he screwed up his courage for one more try. "I like to get along with folks," he said in a kind of scraped-up whine—"especially big taxpayers like your boss, Mr. Spangler, but . . ."

Trimbo, twisting one sardonic eye, said, "He'll be glad to know that," and relapsed into silence.

Jones considered a number of things it would please him to do, but all he actually put into motion was another nervous question. "No," Trimbo said, "I didn't see nobody."

"Then how do you know it was like you said? The horse *could* of—"

"I kin read, can't I?" Trimbo's frown stretched clear across both cheeks. "You debatin' my word?"

Looking into that flattening stare Jones, gulping, gasped for air and like a drowning man mumbled, "No . . . I'm just talkin' . . . just trying to get at the facts."

Trimbo said with a sultry glower: "Any facts that's important you kin git from Geetch," and clamped his jaw like that was the end of it.

He was a hard man to like. Jones mopped his face with the back of a sleeve and thought nostalgically of his years on Rafter when all a man had to do for his wage was ride around after a bunch of cud-chewing cattle.

The sun, climbing higher, beat unmercifully down, and heat came off the ground in waves like a blast from the open door of an oven. Jones' eyeballs felt like they were starting to fry, and, somehow in his misery, he got to thinking about Trimbo's boss, the Number One man at this end of the cactus.

Though he had never swapped as much as two words with Geetch Spangler, he had seen him often enough in town, hellin' round with his crew or sitting in on a game at the Aces Up. It was common knowledge that Spangler had been here when Geronimo and his bronco Apaches had been riding and raiding all through this country.

Geetch had been the first stockman to settle in
these parts and, by that token, had got the best
range, adding to it from time to time other choice
parcels which had taken his eye or dropped into his
lap where others had found the going too rough.
Nor had it yet been forgotten that where natural
causes had proved less than sufficient to discourage
some hardnose on land Spangler wanted, he had
not been above plain-out driving them off.

It got to jouncing around through Jones' ham-
mering skull that perhaps what had happened to
Harley Ferguson out back of Bernagrowt's saddle
shop last night might not be entirely unrelated to
something Geetch wanted.

It was a soul-shaking thought, the kind to wriggle clear down into the very stones and mortar of a
man's foundation.

The sheriff, shuddering, strove valiantly to dis-
claim it, and when this didn't help tried, copiously
sweating, to push it into some far corner of his
mind where he could go about his struggle to sur-
vive in relative comfort, reminding himself that in
his mellowing old age, Spangler's chief concern
and most present source of pride was the stable of
short horses he had boastfully collected.

It was this reminder of Spangler's sprinters that
brought him round to pondering the region's other
mogul, Grisswell, whose headquarters at Gourd &
Vine was the county's finest showplace. And likely
enough a thorn in Geetch's side.

No one—at least in Jones' hearing—had ever

dared hint these two barons were rivals, but you could hardly mention one without including the other, and the pair, in this fashion, had been coupled so long out of deference, self-defense or for whatever reason, that anyone not wearing three-cornered pants must have sensed the general uneasiness progressively growing from such a situation.

Despite his fondness for strong drink and colorful garb, Butterfly Jones, though capable of much foolishness, was sharp enough in his own perverse fashion. He might never have got to the head of his class in the one-room schoolhouse he had briefly attended, but he had his allotted share of marbles and a certain native shrewdness or cunning, which, despite sundry fumbles, had kept him from foundering in the tides of adversity.

To put it bluntly, he hadn't made the scene for twenty-six years with his eyes plumb shut. He could see which side of the bread got the butter and now, adding up what little he knew and piecing out the bare bones with a couple of lively guesses, the notion he came up with was hard to abide.

Hollister Grisswell, with money he had made out of patent medicines, had bought into this country some five years back and proceeded to transform two rundown ranches and their hardscrabble holdings, via artesian wells and considerable irrigation, into about as lush a piece of landscape as could be readily found this side of the Rockies. He and his astonishing experiment made the accomplishments of Spangler look like pretty small potatoes, for despite Geetch's drive and bullypuss methods—not to mention half a lifetime of grinding effort—his own headquarters out at Quarter Circle S, stacked beside Gourd & Vine, seemed more like a huddle of sharecropper shacks than home place of the country's first citizen. All Geetch's sweat had gone into expansion until he'd taken to this folly of collecting race horses. Summing up what he knew and tucking in what he suspected, the conviction Jones hit on was that something had to give—and here he was caught smack in the middle, sheriff of a county hunkered on a powder keg.

It was no dang wonder that tempers were short and Tiedown's town fathers felt so exposed they'd come swarming all over him. Another man in Jones' boots might have pitched in his star.

It would hardly be true to say the thought had not occurred to him. It had been all he could think of the last three or four miles but presently, groaning deep in his belly, he flung it aside. A little authority, if it doesn't plumb spoil him, can do wonders for a man and while, thus far, it hadn't done much for Jones, he was beyond all reasoning reluctant to give it up.

Trimbo, continuing dour and uncommunicative, never once pushed his horse beyond the animal's inclination, which was a sort of lazy shuffle. Heat lay across the dun horizon like smoke, the glare of sky pressed down with the weight of an iron fist. During the past several miles there'd been no sign of a road, but, suddenly coming onto one, Trimbo kneed his mount into it. Jones, eyeing him aghast, cried from an inward quaking: "Say—you gone off your rocker?" Peering ahead again he said, somewhat paler: "This here's the way to Gourd an' Vine!"

Trimbo, following his stare, said, "Damn 'fit ain't."

"What the devil we goin' out there for?"

"Orders was to fetch you. I don't ask Geetch for reasons."

Filled with inner turmoil Jones loosed a couple of gulps and—at least outwardly—subsided. Inside he was a mass of shaken jelly. No matter how he viewed it this trip looked like trouble, the kind of trouble that could get powerful bad and might easily dig someone a hole in short order. Maybe several someones—and it wasn't Geetch Spangler he was worried about.

III

Grisswell's place, when they presently came on it, was enough to squeeze any cowman's heart. It was like peering into the Promised Land, Jones thought, truly awed, as his eyes played over that broad sweep of valley, ringed by sugarloaf hills turned the color of straw. Sunlit greens flecked with cool blue shadows, the stuccoed adobe great house and outbuildings trim and shipshape in a grove of cottonwoods, whose leafy branches waved and twinkled in a breeze alive with the intoxicating smell of this growing profusion of greenery.

Set down as it was in this drab country, with drought's sear hand laying over all else, it might have been taken for a bit of Kentucky snatched from the very heart of bluegrass, its lush meadows bounded by a crisscross of horse fence, the rails painted with loving care the same gleaming white that had been used on the buildings, the whole impression one of peace and plenty.

It just went to show, the sheriff told himself, what a feller could do if he had enough cash. The dude had brought in some white-faced bulls and the calves they saw—even the mother cows—made the kind of stuff Geetch Spangler ran look like the tag-end of nothing, which it was. Any one of those cows would have weighed three of Geetch's, and this grass was only part of the difference.

Trimbo, with his face tied in knots, growled from his wealth of brushpopper's scorn: "Them critters wouldn't last five days on the range!"

"Reckon you got somethin' there. Point is, though, they won't never have to. He's got more'n enough feed for them right on this place. Bet he gets three cuttin's of that alfalfa! Prob'ly got his barns packed plumb to the roofs."

Trimbo flashed him an affronted stare, moved the cud in his cheek and copiously spat. "Let's git over there—there's Geetch now."

Following his look, Jones described the Quarter Circle S owner putting his bay saddler down the horse-fenced lane which crossed the fields like a kind of levee in the direction of the distant tree-shaded headquarters. Reluctantly and with a cold lump forming someplace back of his navel the sheriff kneed his horse after Trimbo. He could think of forty places he would sooner be right now.

But there was no help for it. Trimbo plainly had the bit in his teeth and, while he made no effort to catch up with his boss, he moved right along, and the grip of his features in that gun-bore stare did not encourage Price Jones to hang back.

While they were still some distance short of the house and Spangler was stopping his horse by the steps, a chestnut-haired girl in what sure enough looked to be a man's pair of pants got up out of a chair and, bobbing a nod in the direction of Geetch, disappeared inside the house.

No one had to tell Jones this was Grisswell's daughter; the whole country knew she was home for the summer from that lah-de-dah girls' school she'd been going to at some frothy place they called Buzzard's Bay.

About the time Jones and Trimbo were reining up beside Spangler, who didn't bother to look around or even open his mouth, a portly white-haired geezer in a Palm Beach suit stepped out onto the porch with a welcoming smile. "A fine morning, gentlemen—very fine, indeed. I'm Hollister Grisswell. Come up and make yourselves comfortable. My daughter—"

"What I've got to say," Geetch broke in like he was Moses handing down the Ten Commandments, "can be said well enough right where I'm at."

He was a strapping six-footer, big, well-sprung, and lean with the gauntness of a timber wolf, which, with his yellow eyes, he more than a little resembled, Jones decided, especially the way his head with that ruff of dark hair was hunched forward, and with that glitter of teeth showing behind his peeled lips.

If Grisswell noticed this hostile glare it was scarcely apparent in his courteous pause. "Don't doubt it a bit," he said with a chuckle, "but you'll find these chairs more roomy than a saddle, and my daughter will be along with some refreshments in a jiffy. Won't hurt you to stay long enough to have a drink."

"Didn't come fo' no drink," Spangler threw back gruffly, and the smile on Grisswell's mouth slipped a little. He had a tuft of hair on his chin like a goat, and Jones, chewing his lip, read real strength and considerable more savvy than was generally conceded in the fatty roll of those round and bland cheeks. Geetch, in his usual pile-driver fashion, drove roughshod on, contentiously declaring: "I didn't come over here t' chitchat with women!"

The mood of the man was plainly distrusting and cram-packed with belligerence.

"Well . . ." Grisswell said, "what *are* you here for?"

"We had a horse stole last night an' I mean t' find out what's become of him!"

Grisswell's widening look took in Jones and his badge and dark spots of color burned through his pale cheeks, yet he held himself in with remarkable restraint. "And you imagine he's here?"

"I'm goin' t' damn sure find out!"

The wicked arrogance of it pulled Grisswell's face out of shape, drained the last bit of color from his rigid cheeks. Jones, eyes goggling, hauled his jaw off his chest with an audible groan. Before the dude's resentment could leap out of him in words or he could lunge for a gun, the screen door flung open and the girl appeared with a tray of tall drinks.

She had put on a dress as red as spilled blood with a cameo brooch pulling it tight across her breasts, and with that freshly-brushed hair piled high above white temples, she would at any other moment have caught every eye, so regal, so lovely, was her obviously startled stance.

Jones, profusely sweating and aghast at his own temerity, cried into the breathless core of that hush: "You can't go through a man's property without due process—not, anyways, while *I'm* around!"

It fetched a flash of quick approval from the white-cheeked girl. The stupid, lost-lamb look of Grisswell's stare seemed even more bewildered in the wheel of baffled features; but what it drew from Spangler and his gun-hung hardcase was the cold, unwinking promise of dire action in the near future.

"We don't need no warrant," Geetch Spangler snapped and Grisswell fast recovering his aplomb, waved an airy arm. "Of course you don't," he declared with a dentrifice smile. "We have nothing to hide. Look anywhere you please."

Trimbo considered him with a darker stare as Geetch, reining away from the porch, sent his crow-hopping mount in the direction of the stables and the sprawl of pens beyond. Only Jones, half falling out of his saddle, seemed to feel the need to reach for a drink. Nor did he stand upon politeness in the matter. Snatching a frosted glass from the tray he threw back his head and with no thought but haste emptied it down the bobbing column of his throat.

Grimacing, he dragged a sleeve across his mouth and would have gone after the others had his glance not chanced to catch the girl's look. Her eyes were bright. She shyly smiled and Jones was caught like a fly in the world's oldest web. "It *is* hot, isn't it?" Cathie Grisswell said in the dulcet tones of Eve testing Adam, and her smile reached out to romp through him like a song.

It was the nearest Jones had ever been to her and he sat transfixed, a startled grin on his face like a horticulturist caught up in the wonder of watching some delicate rare flower unfold. All else dropped out of his mind unmissed as the pull of this girl fastened onto his heartstrings.

Her father cleared his throat and swam into Jones' awareness. In the way of an appendage from some forgotten planet Grisswell's arm moved out to pick up a glass, but the spell lingered on until the medicine king's voice, suddenly leaping out of limbo, somewhat impatiently demanded: "What made him think, Sheriff, he would find the horse here?"

It took Jones a minute to break loose from his trance. Even when he found and finally placed the girl's father, he still looked pretty vague and kind of pawed at his face the way a man will trying to rid it of a spider web. "Ugh . . . what's that?"

"Why did the fellow think *I* had his horse?"

Butterfly hated to get back into that. "Search me," he frowned, trying to shrug it away. "Fact of the matter is I didn't even know what in Tophet we was here for till he come right out an' told you. It was Trimbo that come for me, an you could sooner get blood out of a rock than pry anything out of that mule-jawed jigger."

"Still," Grisswell said, as though turning it over, "he must have said *some*thing."

Jones shook his head. "You know as much as I do. All he told me was some guy waltzed into their yard last night, put a halter on this nag, led him to the road, hopped aboard and took off."

Staring past Jones at some notion of his own, Cathie's father took a long pull from his glass. Pushing out his legs, fisting it, "Which horse was it?" he presently asked. "One of those two-twenty wonders he's so overbearingly proud of?"

"Nope," Jones said. "That's what's got him fightin' his hat. Accordin' to Trimbo it was that old geldin' they had been ponyin' 'em with. Trimbo swears the old skate wasn't even worth stable room —kept him outside in a pen. Sounds loco to— what's the matter?"

"A lead horse, you say?"

Grisswell cut the wrapped end from a pale green cigar with a tiny gold knife which he dropped on the table beside the tray the girl had put there, never taking his searching glance from Jones' face. His tongue rolled the weed from one end of his mouth to the other, and, when the sheriff nodded, he put a match to it, vigorously puffing until the swirls of blue smoke hemmed him in like fog.

From this haze his voice said like it was coated with honey: "County fair's coming up on the fifteenth, isn't it?"

Jones couldn't see any possible connection. "What's that got to do with the price of turnips?"

But Grisswell, waving the smoke away, smiled like a man who'd just come into an inheritance. "They'll be holding a race meet in connection with it, won't they?"

"Sure, but—"

"Open to the world?"

Jones, beginning to think this rich dude was even more loco than was generally supposed, stared uncomfortably, finally bobbing his head.

"There's nothing to prevent my entering a thoroughbred?"

"Not if you want to throw your money away."

"Money's only good for what a man can get out of it—"

"You tie into them Steeldusts," Jones said disgustedly, "you won't get enough to buy one of them seegars!"

Grisswell smiled.

He sure was a dope. Cheeks flushed, Jones was minded to wash his hands of it, but a look at Cathie over there, plainly worried, made him say mighty earnest: "Mr. Grisswell, I'm tellin' you it would be plain murder. No thoroughbred yet has ever beat a short horse at the Tiedown county fair —why, these folks around here would go hog wild if you got into it."

"You think Mr. Spangler would make a little bet?"

Jones peered at him and gulped. "They'd take everything you got!"

Grisswell puffed contentedly, blowing out smoke rings like a steam locomotive. Maybe the dang fool *had* took that horse. If he figured to beat them top runners of Geetch's he didn't have enough sense to pound sand down a rat hole!

IV

Jones, with his initial disgust wearing off, had a pitying look wrapped across his cheeks when Spangler and his range boss, throwing hard looks at Grisswell, returned from the stables to sit their mounts in scowling silence.

The dude, Jones reckoned, was too dumb to be worried. Smiling benignly he said: "Now that you've seen for yourselves—"

"All we seen," Geetch snarled, "is that Pete ain't cached in none of them stalls. Don't prove you ain't got him—don't prove a damn thing!"

Grisswell, still in that patronizing tone, declared, "Really, gentlemen, this is pretty ridiculous. I wouldn't waste my time with that kind of horse, but if I *had* happened to want one I could have bought a whole carload and never missed the money. Whatever makes you think I would go out of my way to *steal* one?"

"Don't ask *me* why you done it," Geetch cried testily, rolling his eyes like a sore-back bull. He hauled in a deep breath and, glowering, growled: "If it's trouble you want—"

The dude flipped a hand. "I've heard what happened to some of your neighbors . . . burnings and beatings and broken bones. I'm not afraid of you, Spangler, and I don't intend to be pushed around. Do you understand that?"

Geetch looked like he had been kicked in the face, but more astonished than hurt. Then, abruptly, you could see his blood start to boil. His swollen eyes sank back into his head and he seemed in that moment to have entirely quit breathing. His yellow stare flattened out, turning silvery sharp as a two-pronged fork to reach out and slam Grisswell back against his chair.

In a terrible, half-strangled voice Spangler spoke. "We'll see who's afraid of who," he said, and his words had the slithery sound of a snake. "If that horse ain't put back powerful soon where he come from, somebody's goin' to pick up a skinned nose," and he slapped his mount on the rump, grabbing up his dropped reins.

Grisswell called: "Wait!" and Spangler's raw red cheeks came around. "Well?" he rasped.

Grisswell smiled with his teeth. "Understand you take an inordinate pride in that bunch of scrub broomtails you call running horses . . . even claiming, I hear, you've got the best stock there is. We've got a fair coming along in about ten days. There'll be racing, I suppose?"

"What about it?" Geetch said, truculent.

"I'd like to give this community a chance to discover just how little you really are. I've got a horse I'll run against any nag you own—"

"Hoo hoo!" Geetch jeered. "That stolen pony horse, mebbe?"

"My stallion, Jubal Jo."

Spangler, head to one side, considered him, probably thinking back to the stock he and Trimbo had just looked through in Grisswell's stables. "Never heard of 'im," he scoffed.

The dude curled his lip. "You're hardly likely to have heard of a horse that has not raced. I'll tell you this much: he's by the Kentucky Derby winner, Plaudit, that defeated Lieber Karl."

"Humph. Thoroughbred, eh?"

"That's right."

"You poor deluded fool." Spangler looked his contempt. "You got no more chance'n a June frost at Yuma."

"Then why so reluctant?" Grisswell came back. "If you're so high on those short-winded dogs why not put your money where your mouth is?"

Spangler snorted. "You'd take on Curtain Raiser? Eight Below?"

"Makes no difference to me what you call them. Pick your best."

"How far?" Geetch said, beginning to show caution. "Half a mile?"

Grisswell laughed, saw it darken Geetch's cheeks. "What's your best distance? You're the challenged party. Make it easy on yourself."

Spangler and his range boss exchanged smug looks. "You hard-boot jaspers never learn a thing," Geetch declared, peering down at him, "but a man's a nump not to humor a sucker. If you're bound an' determined t' lose your shirt—an' you're still around come time for them races—I'll take you on for a quarter . . ." he was like a cat with some half-witted mouse—"for *five hundred a side!*" And he winked broadly at Trimbo, openly chuckling at the slick quick way he had snagged this dude in his own piece of twine.

The goddam peckerneck didn't know he was hooked.

Jones winced, embarrassed, as Grisswell in his most insufferable tone wanted to know if that was all Geetch could scrape up. "When I was talking to Gattison—our estimable printer—about the chances of getting out a broadside, the figure I thought of was ten thousand each."

Spangler's eyes boogered out like he'd walked into a wall. The bright satisfaction fell completely away and he stared, mouth agape, unable to grasp this. Even Trimbo sat speechless.

"Those handbills are probably up by now, but of course," Grisswell said with a shake of the head, "if you're not that confident, or plain can't afford it, I suppose we can call the whole thing off. Seems a shame, in a way . . . everybody knowing . . . I suppose they'll figure I froze you out."

Spangler, cheeks livid, drew a shuddering breath and gasped. "Does it hev to all be *cash?*"

Grisswell appeared to mull this over, while everyone breathlessly hung on his words. "I don't think," he smiled, "I'd care to fool with notes, but if you want to put up that Hat Creek range with the buildings and equipment stored at Dead Soldier's Flat and throw in forty tons of top-quality hay in place of hard cash, you've got yourself a deal."

Geetch, as the dude laid down these terms, began to expand like a bad case of bloat. Crammed to the gills with insufferable emotions, the twisting fury raging through his blood seemed as threateningly explosive as a shook-up bottle of blasting oil, and Jones, peering nervously for something to get under, had the look of a man who thought the sky was going to fall.

Spangler couldn't speak he was so furious mad.

Grisswell wasn't done; he had to rub it in. "Sheriff," he said, "I call on you to bear me out. Spangler here, if I understand this right, undertakes on the second day of the Fair to run one of those puddingfoot crossbreds he named a moment ago—Eight Below or the one he calls Curtain Raiser—against my stallion Jubal Jo over a course of four hundred and forty measured yards. If he wins I pay him ten-thousand dollars. If he loses he agrees to sign over to me forty tons of top quality hay, his Hat Creek range, plus the buildings and all equipment presently stored at Dead Soldier's Flat. Is that your understanding?"

Jones, not looking at Spangler, groaned, "Why

don't you leave me out of this?"

The dude, sharply looking Jones up and down, said: "I would hate to believe, as the county's top officer, we've elected a man who's delinquent in his duty. You were here. You heard it. Is my summation correct?"

Jones lugubriously nodded.

Grisswell peered at Geetch. "Do you agree?"

Spangler glared like a dog with a bone. You could almost see the wheels going round.

He was convinced he would win unless his horse fell down. The logic of this was not open to argument—time and again Geetch had seen it proved. The tall, weedy thoroughbred, no matter how fast at bloodhorse distances, was a mighty poor risk against the short, chunky Steeldust in any all-out dash. It took most of those hardboots the biggest part of an eighth just to get up their steam, while the bred-for-it short horse reached maximum velocity inside three jumps.

The deal, as set up, gave Spangler all the advantages, and by that token it looked too good to be true. It was this that kept digging him. It didn't seem likely the dude could be such a chump. There had to be some kind of hanky-panky, some slick piece of trickery tucked away someplace. Nothing else made sense, and it worried him plenty. He stood to lose ten sections of the best graze he had.

The man's uneasy suspicions were plain even to Jones.

"Well?" Grisswell spoke impatiently. "No one's forcing you, Spangler. You can still back down if you don't mind folks knowing—"

Greetch, beside himself, swore like a mule skinner. The dude had him over a barrel. He couldn't back down, not with everybody knowing it. He'd be laughed clean out of the goddam county! The look on the face of that stupid sheriff warned him how swiftly news of that sort would fly. He was a gaffed fish and knew it.

"All right," he snarled. "You're goin' t' know, by Gawd, you been in a horse race!"

Grisswell nodded. "There's just one more thing. Let's have it clearly understood that if for any reason this match is called off, or one of the horses fails to run when the time comes, the stake of the one who defaults is forfeit."

Geetch looked a long while and mighty hard at Grisswell before, with a grimace, he jerked his bitter face at Trimbo. "Let's git outa here," he grumbled.

V

But just as they were wheeling and Jones—freed at last from his clutching dread—was shakenly reaching for a first dull breath, Spangler growled, twisting around to peer back across Trimbo. "You taken root there, Sheriff?"

The lump so prominent in Butterfly's neck popped up and down convulsively while he hung, bulge-eyed, like a fish out of water. His chin sort of trembled like the lip of a stove-up horse, but nothing came out that a man could hear or see.

It was Cathie who cried brightly, "But he can't go *now!* He promised to stay for lunch and it's practically on the table!"

And her father fondly said, pushing up with his rich man's smile, "You'll find a promise to Cathie about as easy to wriggle out of as a straitjacket, my boy. And you did promise—remember?"

Jones, finding his voice, gulped, "Dang if I didn't," and, dropping his reins, commenced to flounder toward the porch.

Through sweat-soaked shirt he could feel the burn of Spangler's stare. Any moment the man, always unpredictable, might do something drastic, and even though he didn't Jones, with dry throat, had a frightening hunch he had not heard the last of this. But he went doggedly on after the girl's lissome figure, trailing her through the pulled-open screen and into the cool and ornate security of the medicine king's home.

Through the myriad wonders of a shuttered withdrawing room, Cathie led him to an elegant horsehair sofa and, seating herself beside him—at a properly virtuous distance of course—said through the shine of a tremendous smile, "I don't know what you must think of me, telling such a fib. You didn't really *want* to go back with them, did you?"

The gist of her rhetorical question entirely escaped him—all he heard was the tinkle of her mission-bell voice, soothing and soft as the wings of young doves. He felt queerly lightheaded staring into her eyes, permeated with the dizzy sort of wonder that overtakes converts on their pilgrimage to mecca. Perhaps he had been in the sun too long. He gulped and stammered, foolishly grinning. She was thrilled, he could see, just to be in his company, even crossing her legs to lean a little closer.

"I think sheriffs," she said, peering up into his face, "must be terribly brave. I almost swooned when you stood up to that horrible Geetch Spang-

ler, daring him to search our ranch without a
warrant—but I was proud of you, too. Imagine
him thinking we would take his old nag! As though
Daddy would have any use for it. Ugh!"

It did sound loco but Jones, recollecting, fought
up out of his trance to say, "Accordin' to Trimbo—"

"That man's got rocks in his head!"

"Umm . . . well, there ain't nothin' wrong with
his eyes that I've noticed. He claims the tracks
headed straight for this ranch."

"Claims! Did *you* see any tracks?"

"No, but—"

"Of course you didn't, or anyone else. The whole
thing's preposterous! I think Spangler wants to
take over this ranch; he resents Daddy bitterly—he
can't stand the thought of someone else being important. Look what he did to the rest of his neighbors—I've heard the stories!" Her eyes took hold
of him. "Have you killed many people?" she asked
low and breathless.

"Well—no," Jones confessed, swallowing uncomfortably.

But her look said she knew he was just being
modest. "I've heard about Masterson and Moss-
man, all those others. A man has to have a great
deal of experience, my father says, nerves of steel
and be a dead shot before he can hope to be elected
sheriff." She considered him intensely. "Would
you do something for me?"

Jones, badly rattled, stared aghast. "You—You
mean—*kill* somebody?"

35

"Silly! Please be serious," she said, gripping his arm. "I want you to write in my autograph album; I'm collecting signatures of famous people."

Batting those pansy eyes at him again, "I want *yours*," she cried prettily, jumping up to hang over him. The hand she extended was warm, firm, and astonishingly urgent. There was a fragrance about her reminiscent of crushed violets, and something indescribably exciting left its bright track across the turn of her glance. In that bent-forward face her enormous eyes looked weirdly blue-purple. Jones was briefly reminded of Concord grapes; then she tugged at him harder. "It's in my room—come on!" she impatiently whispered.

Tipped toward him like that he got to see more of Cathie than was generally discernible. His cheeks turned hot, his head pounded fiercely, yet he was not without a rather horrid sort of antici-patory tingle as he allowed her to pull him to his feet.

He wasn't rightly sure just what she had in mind, but despite his jumbled notions he was immensely relieved when, before she could snake him into deeper water, a frozen-faced butler arrived to an-nounce lunch.

Jones stumbled after him, copiously sweating.

Back in town some three hours later, having cared for his horse, Tiedown's new sheriff—tired, disgruntled, and about as uneasy in the churn of his thoughts as a one-legged paper hanger fresh out of stickum—stepped into the trapped heat of his two-by-four office to find it filled with the shapes of waiting men.

He didn't care for the way they looked at him, and when Bud Flancher growled, "Where the hell you been?" Jones knocked the top off his can of private cusswords. "I been busy," he flared, "tryin' to find a stole horse—an' if you got to know more you better jump on your bronc an' lope out for a gab with the brass-collar dog of these here localities! The mogul who figures he pays most of my salary an' expects me t' leap through hoops when he whistles!"

The hotel man edged back with his mouth flapping, and a kind of frozen hush seemed to grip the whole push except T. Ed Gretchen who, being town banker with a safe full of plasters, considered himself immune to the disasters which frequently haunted his less affluent depositors.

"You've been to Quarter Circle S?"

"I've been to Gourd and Vine, too—an' what's been happenin' round this burg don't hold a patch to the trouble that's buildin' between Spangler an' Grisswell. Here," Jones growled, thrusting a torn and badly wrinkled broadsheet under the banker's quivering nose—"read that! An' if that ain't enough, grab hold of your hat. Geetch has practically accused that confounded dude of stealin' the horse Trimbo says was made off with!"

Shocked gasps met this news; but Gretchen, never looking at the paper Jones had passed him, said above the panicked groans: "I believe the county seat has first call on the professed abilities for which you were elected. The commissioners when they visited you this morning handed down an ultimatum. What have you done about it?"

Jones said sullenly: "How many legs you think I got?"

"Results is what we're interested in. We want to know what you've done about Ferguson's—"

"Who's Harley Ferguson," Jones demanded, "that every clock should stop because—"

Gretchen said with vast patience: "Just a two-bit leaser trying to make a winning from a played-out hole. It's not *who* he was we're concerned about but *what happened to him* and *where*. You go off all day tearing around after some horse while murder stalks the streets of—"

"We ain't goin' t' stand for it!" Flancher broke in, furious. "It's a matter of public safety!" he cried. "Not a one of us is safe—man, woman or child, while some loco killer—"

"I can't be more than one place at one time!"

"What we're tryin' to pound through your stupid head," Eph Wilson, the Mercantile's owner, snarled, "is, your place is *here!* Us merchants are paying for police protection."

"Yeah," mimicked Jones, "two cents on the dollar! That'll buy you enough for about three snorts!"

Eyeing them scathingly he said, fed up: "I got no reason to speak up for Geetch Spangler, but year in an' year out he pays more taxes than all you counter-jumpers piled in one heap. He's got a *right* to expect some return, by grab. Here—take your damn tin," he cried, ripping off his badge. "Shove it up your you-know-what!"

They peered, drop-jawed, incredulous and aghast, eyes looking like they would flop off their cheekbones. "B-but you *can't* do that . . ." the banker gasped, jowls quivering. "You swore to up-hold—"

"I didn't know then what a cheapjack bunch of fritterin' old women was goin' to be hangin' over me all the time. An' I never give out t' buck up ag'in *murder!*"

"You reckon we pay out eighty a month for you to set on your prat and buck Old Crow? Flancher looked for two cents like he'd take hold of Jones.

But, somewhere among the dark crosses of office and frightening glimpses of things to come, Price Jones' spinal column must have picked up some starch. "There's your badge," he cried—"put it on, why don'tcha, an' see how far *you* git!"

In the hush that reached out while he paused to grab breath, the rest of them stood like they were hacked out of wood, and damned poor wood at that.

He showed his scorn in a jeering grin. "Someone around here is goin' to have to face up to what's about t' come down on you. Take a squint at that paper Gretchen's wavin' around. You beller about what happened to that leaser. One stiff ain't *nothin'*; git your eyes open, man! You're liable, before this is done, t' have 'em stacked in the alleys three an' four deep."

Grabbing the paper the burly saloonman spread it out. "Cripes amighty! Account of a *horse race?*" he said in disgust.

"Account of what it can lead to when one of 'em gits beat. You don't see it?" Jones stared. "Spangler an' Grisswell. Biggest men in this county. How many, you reckon, can stay outa this when them two gits on the prod for sure? The feud they're hatchin' can split this county end for end; it sure won't be no place for women an' kids then."

Eph Wilson and Gretchen turned dubious, nervous; even Flancher began to show signs of worry. Bernagrowt anxiously eyed the banker. "He just might be right. Remember how it was that time Geetch took after them Collison brothers. . . ."

And the storekeeper said in his E-string whine, "Maybe, if he was to raise him twenty dollars, Butterfly here could be persuaded to stay on—"

Jones, glowering, said: "Do I look like a *fool?* You think twenty bucks would make up for gittin' planted?"

Flancher growled: "You was willin' enough when there wasn't no trouble. What the hell are you, a man or a mouse?"

Jones didn't like what he saw on their faces. He didn't like any part of this. But if he quit the job now the whole country would figure he'd been scared off—he could see it in their eyes. *No*body would hire him, not around here. "Well . . ." he said, wavering, and T. Ed Gretchen stepped into the breach.

"Tell you what we'll do," he said, and pinned the

star back on Butterfly's shirt. "We'll up you another twenty a month and give you a deputy. That's fair enough, isn't it, to keep on with a job you've already sworn to do?"

Jones, far from sure, edgily nibbled his lip. He considered the advantages. "All right," he grumbled, "but no more delegations. I want it understood I'm to have a free hand."

VI

Trouble was, he figured out later, a man—hating to be set up for any kind of patsy—dislikes even more to seem an out-and-out coward.

But nothing had changed. No part of the ruckus he had sensed shaping up appeared any less touchy on sober reflection. Sure, he'd been upped twenty bucks a month to stay with it—drawing now the equivalent of a foreman's wage—plus the further concession of a deputy to work off his frustrations on; but he was still uncomfortably nagged by the suspicion Ed Gretchen and them others had someway jobbed him.

He went out for his supper and when he got back the office lamp had been lighted. Through the dust clinging thick to the cobwebby window he could see someone hunched over the desk with a pencil.

More grief, he reckoned, yanking open the sagging screen; and stopped dead upon discovering it was the county coroner. "Well, fan my saddle! Ain't you kinda premachoor?"

The man at the desk brushed a hand across his jaw. Eyes that were almost black came up, peering at Jones and plainly not seeing him.

"I ain't dead *yet*," Butterfly snorted. Harold Terrazas had always made Jones a little uncomfortable. On top of everything else he found it hard to understand how any man with real bone in his spinal column could be content to be doodling around with a pencil all the time. Some of the animals he drew looked likely enough to get right up and walk off the paper. You had to give him that.

Jones grumbled: "You hear about me gittin' a raise?" and pushed out his chest, dragging a sleeve across the shine of his star before going over to flop on his cot. "Just let 'em know if they figured to keep me, they had to git off my back an sweeten the pot. Them fellers ain't dumb," he told the Mexican, nodding. "They could see plain enough—"

"Yeah. Twenty dollars worth. You sure hung it on them."

Something about the way that was said yanked a closer look from the long arm of the law. "That wasn't all they give me," Jones grumbled, bristling. He couldn't think why he should defend himself but that melancholy stare brought back all his doubts. He cried, almost snarling: "They even throwed in a deputy!"

"I know. Me." Terrazas sighed.

Jones, feeling better, had got as far as reaching for a vindicated breath before the jolt in those words caught up with him. "You!"

For a moment there, flapping up off that cot, you might have reckoned he had picked up a coral snake. He had that waxen look that sometimes grabs onto faces at the reading of a will.

"But they can't do that!" he cried.

"What I told them. They done it anyhow."

"But you're the coroner, man!"

"My very words. You know what that son-vabitch banker said? Said they was giving me the chance to work out my 'indebtedness'—like it was *my* fault no one ever dies around here! There isn't a grateful bone in that bugger's whole body." He heaved a shuddering sigh.

And then, remembering, "Even had to buy me a gun, and all they'll put up toward transportation is the shoe bills and grain cost, and not even that unless I'm out on the road."

His well-padded frame quivered, like jelly. "Chihuahua!" he groaned, then looked up to say, thoughtfully, "You're wrong about Spangler."

Jones' chin kind of set after the way of a stubborn mule, and a bad look came out of him. "What d'ya mean, wrong?"

"I don't think he's—Why would he want to be kicking up trouble?"

"Why does a hen cross a road?" the sheriff scowled. "It's his nature, that's why. When you've put up with the kind of things I cut my teeth on—"

"I know the guy's pushy. Gritty as fish eggs rolled in sand—and *proud!* I'll give you that, but he's in mighty poor flesh to be courting ambition. He's had three bad years, and this drought—"

"He don't worry about drought! Why should he? He's got every waterhole sewed up—"

"And most of them so dry you couldn't make mud if you spit all day." Terrazas appeared to have given much thought to this, and said now earnestly: "He's got no patent to the Verdigris River and Grisswell's straddled smack above him, both sides. You ever think about that?"

Jones, snorting, said, "All he's ever *done* is make trouble! You can't git around that! An' Trimbo . . . what you reckon . . ."

"Trimbo could be part of it, maybe," the coroner conceded with an unsure frown, "but there's more to this than Trimbo." He considered Jones darkly. "You must have heard he's been losing beef?"

"Nothin' to it," Butterfly scoffed. "You're talkin' about that hill crowd west of him. If there was anythin' in it he'd of clumb all over 'em." Jones looked his disgust. "You think he'd hold still for a thing like that!"

"Don't guess he could help himself."

"That'll be the day! Any time that ol' wolf—"

"He's an old man, Price. Half his crew's quit." Terrazas leaned forward earnestly and, with Jones saturninely eyeing him, said: "It's the truth. Six of his hands pulled out on today's noon stage; whole town's been talking."

"Musta been fired then. Man don't quit when he's hired out to Spangler. Not without . . . The noon stage, eh? They musta sneaked off while him an'—"

"Flip Farley claimed there haven't any of them been paid in the past four months. Geetch has been passing out I.O.U.'s. You can ask Ed Gretchen— he was standing right there."

Jones stared with his mouth open.

"Geetch must be in a pretty bad way—for cash, anyhow," Terrazas said, straightening. "And this wager . . ." He got out one of the broadsheets Gattison had printed. "You think if he could get hold of cash he'd have put up that Hat Creek range of his? Who started this race talk anyway—him?"

"Well, no," Jones admitted.

"And here's something else. I went around to the Aces Up after those boys left and had a talk with the barkeep. It's true, right enough. Spangler's crew has been passing Geetch's paper. Barkeep said his boss had put a stop to it, and I got the same story at the Purple Cow." He peered at Jones darkly.

Jones tugged his mustache, looking beat and worried.

"Like you," Terrazas said, "I think we're in for a squall, I can't help feeling someone's *nursing* this feud, but I don't believe it's Geetch. I think it's someone outside who's got his plans laid for a killing. Someone," he said grimly, "who knows the spot Spangler's in and not only where to jab him but—"

Boots crossed the stoop with an urgent *ching* of rowels. The screen was yanked open and disclosed the excited lamplit faces of Shores, Grisswell's ranch manager. Ignoring Terrazas, Shores cried at Jones: "You better get out to Gourd and Vine, Sheriff—someone out there is trying to kill Mr. Grisswell!"

VII

Jones gaped like someone who'd been poked in the stomach. Grisswell's man, swinging around, pinned Terrazas with an exasperated stare. "Can't he hear? What's the matter with him?"

The coroner, with Latin eloquence, shrugged.

"Hell!" Butterfly growled, abruptly coming to life. "When'd it happen? Who done it? Is the old fool dead?"

Shores' eyes bulged like grapes beneath the snap-brim hat. "He . . . ah . . . wasn't when I left. . . ." Florid cheeks mottling to a fish-belly white, he said in half-strangled outrage; "I'll thank you, my good man, to employ a civil tongue. Mr. Hollister Grisswell is a person of considerable substance, a pharmaceutical wizard, a—"

"I didn't ask for his pedigree."

"My dear fellow," Shores said, "we're discussing

a Genghis Khan of the financial world who cannot be dismissed with a wave of the hand. As a man of vast interests, one of your largest taxpayers and most influential—"

Jones made a vulgar noise with his mouth and the other man, shocked, drew himself to his full height. Looking down his nose he declaimed with umbrage: "I would advise . . ." and, faltering, backed off as Jones came toward him like a runaway freight, fists doubled, jaws grinding audibly.

"Now you listen to me? All I been gittin' all day is advice! I don't want any more so choke off the blat! I left your place at two. Then what happened?"

Eldon Shores in his scissorsbill hat and tweedy plus-fours had been fetched West from Chicago. He was scoffingly referred to around Tiedown as a "buggy boss," as foreign to his element as a cow is to bloomers. He was a man from the world of papers and figures. Appalled by the crudeness of his present surroundings, his defense was contempt, the arrogance of patronage. But faced with the cantankerous look of Price Jones this facade began to crumble.

Shaken, he said: "I don't know. I was in my office going over the books. I—I'm afraid I rather lost track of the time. I heard a shot. It seemed to come from outside. As I ran into the yard there was a second shot, the kind of flat crack you get from a rifle, then a thudding of hoofs beyond the big barn."

He swallowed nervously. "I dashed into the

stables. Miss Cathie appeared in the door to the pens. 'It's Daddy!' she said. 'Someone's trying to kill him! Oh—hurry?' she cried, and I dashed toward the—"

"Was he hit?"

"Well . . . no," Shores replied with an irascible look, "but one of our horses—"

"Then all you're doin' is guessin'," Jones said. "Sounds a heap more like somebody was tryin' to throw a fright into him."

"Mr. Grisswell isn't easily frightened."

"He honestly thinks this jigger tried to—?"

"I suggest you talk to Mr. Grisswell himself. He said something about the Lord apparently having more work for him; it was a mighty near thing. One of those bullets tore the sleeve of his shirt. The other nicked his left ear—"

"I thought you said he wasn't hit!"

"It looked more a burn than a hit, hardly broke the skin. But," Shores cried indignantly, "if it had struck any closer it would have torn off his jaw!"

Butterfly, grunting, scooped up his hat. "Mind the store," he told Terrazas.

Grisswell's ranch manager, starting to put out a hand and then—considering Jones' look—deciding against it, said, "Where are you off to?" But the sheriff, jaws clamped, shoved open the door and, without bothering to answer, departed.

By the wash of the stars it was nearing ten o'clock when he picked up the lights of Gourd & Vine. Tired and irritable, it came over him now he had probably put in this ride for nothing. He could stay over, of course, and have a look in the morning. If it wasn't so late he could have chinned with the girl—not that the prospect was unadulterated joy, still you had to admit she'd gone out of her way to . . . Jones, groaning, rode on to pull up by the porch. She was the only millionaire's daughter he had ever been close to, and she was sure some different than he had figured she'd be. Just thinking about her put him in a cold sweat.

The bunkhouse was dark. All the lights he had seen appeared to come from the house. He sat there a moment, then called, "Anybody home?"

He heard steps and then Cathie's form was pressed against the lamp-lit screen. Her lifted hands closed round her face and for a couple of seconds she stood wholly still, peering. "Who—who is it?" she called in a thin, frightened voice.

Butterfly gulped. "Price Jones," he said, and she flung open the screen to hurry prettily out and stop at the top of the steps, widely staring, while Jones' pounding heart threatened to burst from his chest.

"Is it really you?" And when he said that it was, and got out of the saddle, she ran down the steps to bury her face against his chest. He could feel her shake through the moan of her sobs. Over her head Price Jones scowled fiercely. "There, there," he grumbled, clumsily patting her.

"I thought you *never* would come!" she wailed. But she got hold of herself quick enough when he said, "You know? I been thinkin'. Be a fine how-de-do an' six hands around if someone from this place—that prissy-mouthed Shores or some other hired hand—actually did lift Geetch's horse."

She pulled back from him, stiff as a touched gopher. "Are you out of your mind!"

The stab of her eyes was like polished glass, then a bark of a laugh tumbled out of her and she straightened, hands poking her hair, to say ruefully, "I declare you had me going for a moment. Where *is* Mr. Shores—he hasn't been hurt, has he?"

"He'll be along, I expect. I'd like to talk to your father."

"You'll have to wait till tomorrow then. I gave him a hot toddy and put him to bed. Poor lamb, this thing really took it out of him . . . the shock, and all. He looked awful; but I can show you the place if you have to get back. The tracks, I mean."

Jones rubbed his jaw. She looked at him brightly. "We'd be glad to have you stay; there's plenty of room in the bunkhouse. We don't keep a big crew. A place like this, irrigated and fenced . . . just a matter of rotation; about all the hands have to do is push levers."

"You know where the shot were fired from?"

"That little hill with the hackberries just above the pens."

"Well . . . if it wouldn't be too much bother?"

"No bother at all. Come on," she said, reaching out for his hand.

She found a lantern in the barn and when Jones put a match to it several of the kept-up horses softly nickered and one, a big black, restively pawed for attention. "That's Jubal," she laughed. "I'm afraid he's spoiled rotten."

Jones followed her through a far door that opened onto the corrals. "Did Eldon tell you one of our horses was killed? One of our bred mares in foal to Jubal Jo," Cathie said. "She'd been having some trouble. That's why Daddy was out here. And this is where they were," she said, pointing, "in that corner there by the tank."

Butterfly held up the lantern. "What happened to the mare?"

"She's dead." Cathie shuddered. "One of those bullets that were meant for Daddy—"

"I mean, where is she now?"

"Oh. Eldon had the crew bury her. This heat . . ."

"All right." Jones couldn't see that it made much difference; he couldn't learn anything from eyeing a dead horse. "Let's git up on that hill." He did think, though, they might have waited till he saw it.

He said, walking beside her, "You have much trouble finding—?"

"Not too much. One of the hands saw the fellow when he was trying to get away."

"*Saw* him?" Jones stopped.

"Not really. Just a glimpse as the man went tearing off through the brush—over beyond our south fence, you know."

Jones eyed her sharply. "Toward Spangler's Hat Creek range?"

"Well, yes, I suppose so . . . if that's what's south

of us. I don't really know. I've been so upset about Daddy—"

"Anyone pick up his sign?"

"The boy that caught that glimpse of him tried. He left a pretty plain trail till he climbed from the wash. When the tracks ran out in that lava spill Joe followed them back up here to this hill, which is how we discovered where the shots had come from."

Puffing a little from the exertion of the climb they moved into the trees. This was more a clump than any real kind of woods, scarcely shoulder high, a tiny jungle of canes topped by splotches of foliage. Jones, boring deeper, holding up the lantern, picked out the drygulcher's nest from a trail of broken branches. He found three cigarette stubs, hand-rolled, and one ejected cartridge case, but the ground was too hard for any useful prints.

Pocketing the shell he shoved on through with his eyes peeled for horse tracks. He found tracks, two sets, so inextricably mixed not even a Chinese lawyer would have been able to unravel them. He would have liked to have booted that Joe clean to Halifax. But swearing wasn't going to help him any.

Rejoining the girl he told her grumpily, "That hand of yours that went to look at them tracks did everything but roll in 'em."

She said defensively, "He was just trying to help—"

"He helped, all right. We might as well go back. There ain't nothing here."

On the way to the house he remained uncommonly silent. At the porch, about to swing up, he said gruffly, "You want I should send the doc out t' look at him?"

"At Daddy?" He thought she sounded sort of astonished. Then she said, darkly sober, "He isn't going to like it, but maybe it *would* be a good idea. If he'll come out in the morning . . ."

"I'll send him," Jones grunted, and went into the saddle. "I'm obliged for your help." He lifted his hat and put the horse into motion, somehow glad she hadn't seen him pick up that shell.

He twisted around once in the drive to find her watching, just where he'd left her. Seeing her lift a hesitant hand, Jones waved back, prickled with goose bumps. Then, remembering that shell, he cursed under his breath.

The tinny sound of an off-key piano tinkled up from the street while he stabled his mount. Bone-weary, disgusted, bad in need of a drink, Jones was strongly minded to go tie one on. Instead, he went dragging his spurs down the echoing planks, glumly bound for the jail, dismally filled with the look of a town he had never seen soberly before at 3 A.M.

The office, though dark, was neither empty nor quiet. Snores filtered raucously through the baggy, patched screen, and he pulled up, to sourly peer once again toward the Purple Cow before, grunting, he yanked open the squeaking door and let it bang.

A series of spluttering snorts came from the cot and a shape pushed darkly up and grew still behind the metallic rasp of a cocked six-shooter. "Oh, fer cripes sake," Jones growled testily, "light the lamp."

In the yellow glow Terrazas scratched himself and pushed an irritable hand through his disheveled hair. "Did you have to get me up in the middle of the night?"

Jones, saying nothing, set the cartridge case down on the desk beside the lamp. Terrazas in his long-handled drawers bent nearer. His eyes came up sharply. "That dude ain't dead is he?"

Butterfly, irascibly shaking his head, said, "Look at that damn thing!"

Terrazas curiously picked the shell up, turning it about in his competent fingers. "Buffalo gun. What's the matter with it?"

"Well," Jones said, "it come from where that drygulcher stood. Fired from a rifle chambered for the .45-120-550—a *Sharps!* You know anybody around here besides Geetch that's got one?"

VIII

During the weeks that followed Jones got nowhere at all. For all he and Terrazas accomplished
they might as well have been out punching cows.
Separately and sometimes together the sheriff and
Terrazas conversed with a gamut of people, but
nothing they discovered appeared to advance their
investigations by one substantial fact. They failed
to unearth a single lead which might disclose the
identities of the three masked rowdies who had
stuck up the Purple Cow. They got nowhere with
the killing of Harley Ferguson, and the more they
cudgeled their brains about Spangler the blacker he
looked.

After quitting Gourd & Vine the day Jones had
stayed on for lunch, Geetch could have easily
turned back, or sent Long Creek Trimbo to trigger
the pair of slugs which had dropped Grisswell's

mare. Terrazas took the view that, whoever it was, all they'd really intended was to throw a good fright into Grisswell; but Jones, though he nodded, was a long way from sure.

Both Geetch and Trimbo had sat in on that Aces Up poker game which had put such a tempting load in Ferguson's pockets. Butterfly had not questioned either man, not wanting, he told Terrazas, to tip his hand. But the coroner, sounding out others, discovered it to be the general opinion that once the game had broken up, the pair from Quarter Circle S had left straightaway for the stable to get their horses and take off. Actually, it appeared, they had left the saloon some fifteen minutes ahead of the leaser.

Just for the hell of it Jones had dropped around to shoot the breeze with the liveryman, and almost gave himself away when he was told: "No Spangler horses was here. The night you're talkin' about that Quarter Circle S bunch had their broncs all tied along the street. In front of Bernagrowt's shop, I think it was."

Considerably exercised, Butterfly had Terrazas talk to the Dutchman. Yes, the saddlemaker said, six or seven Spangler-branded mounts had been racked before his place. He couldn't say how long they'd remained there but they were still out front when he'd gone home at eight o'clock.

Jones went around to have a look at the hotel guest book. Flancher himself was on duty and, at the sheriff's request, pushed it over for Jones to leaf through. Flancher was nobody's fool. Lowering his voice he said, eyeing the date, "If it's Geetch you're figuring to look up, he was here."

Jones flattened his lips. "All night?"

"As to that I couldn't say. The bed was used. That's all I can tell you. I didn't see him come in. I didn't see him leave."

Jones, enjoining silence, thanked the man for his help and, like a kid going barefoot across sun-blistered tarmacadam, took a somewhat abrupt and gingerly departure. Flancher may have spoken straight from gospel, but Spangler's name had not been on that page.

Though they worried it like two dogs with a bone, neither the sheriff nor his deputy could turn up one soul who would admit to having seen Harley Ferguson alive after leaving the Aces Up. About the only unswervable thing they pinned down was that Geetch had been playing with paper in the game and had "sure dropped a bundle."

They fooled around for a while with the reasonable theory that the theft of Spangler's horse, the Purple Cow holdup and Ferguson's murder might be wholly unrelated rather than stemming from a single mind, but this proved too much for Jones to swallow.

"You're probably right," Terrazas reluctantly grumbled, holding off to scan through half-shut lids the sketch he'd just made of the disgruntled sheriff. "Besides," he said, sighing, "it doesn't take into account what happened to Gattison."

"Oh, my gosh!" Jones exploded. "You reckon that's part of it?"

The coroner tossed aside his handiwork. "We'd be stupid to overlook it. Putting that print shop out of commission probably kicked off this crime wave." He frowned. "A logical opener. It put the paper out of business. And it's the kind of thing Geetch would do."

Butterly shoved baffled hands through his hair. "He's violent enough to of done it. But somehow I never did figure him for smart. A feller that would throw all he has into horses—"

"He's like an old cranky wolf with one foot in a trap. He'll do—"

"Hell's fire!" Jones exclaimed, jumping up. "Stay here," he cried, sloshing on his hat, and lit out like a scorpion had crawled up his pants' leg.

The screen banged shut. Terrazas winced. "Gringos!" he said, wrinkling his nose. Then he thought of his wife and the fine tasty supper she'd be sure to have waiting. He took a glance at his watch. Then, leaning back with a comfortable sigh, he parked his feet on Jones' desk and, in defense against flies, dropped the hat over his face.

All over town they were talking about the fair and the stupidity of dudes who ridiculously imagined a thoroughbred stood any chance against Steeldusts and Travelers at anything under a full half mile. No one liked Grisswell, and not many would have crossed the street for Geetch, but at least he was a product of their environment. A mogul, to be sure, but a man who had come up from nothing. And he was reasonably predictable.

Grisswell and most of his help were outsiders. His wealth and his ways made them vaguely uncomfortable. In a manner of speaking they could take pride in Spangler, but Grisswell they resented. So all the smart money was down on Geetch's horse, and the barkeeps were doing a splendiferous business.

The dude's buggy boss had let it be known his employer would cover every nickel put up and they were coming in droves to get in on this gold rush. The man was fair game and everybody figured to get a stake from his disaster.

The fair was due to open tomorrow night and already the town was packed to the gills with folks who'd come early to get in on the fun. Flancher's hotel was crammed solid and every rooming house was filled. Jones, on his tour, encountered a mort of strange faces, and not all of these were men.

Something had turned over in Butterfly's mind when the coroner had likened Geetch to a cranky old wolf with one foot in a trap. There still wasn't the least bit of evidence to connect anyone with the theft of Spangler's pony horse. There wasn't a smidgen of proof the dude had been back of it despite Trimbo's claim the tracks had led toward his ranch. But Grisswell had certainly bamboozled Spangler into agreeing to this race, no two ways about that, and had cunningly prodded him into putting up acreage he couldn't afford to lose.

It wasn't the why of this that kept nagging Jones —who could account for a dude's preposterous notions? It was Spangler that bothered him—

Spangler's volatile, oft-demonstrated temper.
Geetch, if he were desperate enough, would balk at
precious little. He was not, Jones thought, the kind
to pass up any bets and if he got it in his head there
was a chance of Grisswell winning he would take
whatever steps seemed most likely to cinch things
for himself. *Even to tampering with Grisswell's
horse.* And there were plenty of jaspers he could
hire to take care of this.

Some such dark purpose may have been the
basis of the dude's condescending confidence. The
more Jones considered this the more alarmed he
grew.

On the face of things there appeared very little
likelihood of any thoroughbred running away from
one of Geetch's short horses, particularly Eight
Below or that flea-bitten mare he called Curtain
Raiser. Both were horses Geetch had paid hand-
some prices for, veteran campaigners in the
roughest kind of company, horses he'd been beaten
by and then had gone out and bought to make sure
it couldn't happen again. By local standards nothing could catch them.

But Grisswell must certainly have known all this.
Any feller who'd amassed a fortune from nostrums
was not likely to be as big a fool as Grisswell
looked. The man had to be convinced he could
win.

Jones, tramping the town darkly, completely out
of sorts with its holiday mood, believed there had
to be an angle hidden somewhere. Grisswell had
pushed this thing onto Spangler, setting it up like

an arrogant chump, leading with his chin, practically asking to be fleeced. And yet the way in which he'd maneuvered Spangler's acceptance was slicker than slobbers when you hauled off to take a good look at it.

The sheriff, at this point, was reluctantly minded to get on his horse, ride out and have another go at interrogating the man. Not that he imagined anything definitely helpful would come from it. He found Grisswell pretty near as hard to take as Geetch and his bullypuss ramrod. But he couldn't just sit here and wait for that pair to shove a chunk under hell.

Still scowling, he was about to go fetch his horse when he happened to notice Charlie "Rockabye" Mullins backing a spring wagon up against the loading platform of Eph Wilson's Mercantile. Mullins was Geetch Spangler's trainer and had the earned reputation of knowing all there was to be discovered about bangtails.

Though she dressed and frequently employed a brand of language more natural in a man than was generally reckoned proper in a maiden lady, she hadn't stayed with that status on account of being shortchanged when the shapes were passed around. In a rough shirt and jeans a feller didn't need glasses to be aware that she was sure female enough.

Nobody denied that she had had a hard life, orphaned at ten, forced to fend for herself amongst a bunch of rough ranch hands. There was scarcely any basis for comparison between her and, for in-

stance, Cathie Grisswell; but a man couldn't help
noticing some of the more manifest differences.
Jones recalled the rich fragrance, the crushed violets' smell of the medicine king's daughter, or the
intimate cadences of Cathie's hushed voice. He
couldn't forget those prickles of excitement.

You'd think a girl, time she got in spittin' distance of thirty, would have figured out some way
to get herself up more attractive. Charlie Mullins,
he guessed, plain didn't give a damn. Hair skinned
back from her ears in that sloppy bun!

Butterfly, peering across the heads of the crowd,
wore a concerned and somewhat dubious expression, the look of a kid caught stealing apples.

He'd swapped words with her before, had even
taken her to a couple of hoedowns and once had
been brash enough to bid in her box lunch, but, in
common with most of the unattached males, had
found her tongue a little sharp for his taste.

Kind of gritting his teeth he thought of that long
ride between him and Geetch's place and began to
use his elbows. Approaching the wagon, careful
not to stare as she climbed down off her perch, he
broke out a smile and said with an assumption of
heartiness; "Ain't seen you in a flock of Sundays.
What's brought you t' town a day ahead of the
fair?"

Pushing a wisp of mousy hair off her cheek, her
clay-marble eyes considered his flushed cheeks
without noticeable change. "Any special reason
you'd be wanting to know?"

"Cripes," he said, nettled, "I was just makin' talk."

"Humph!" she sniffed as though she found it presumptuous, and was turning away when Jones, clenching his fists, kissed caution good-bye, angrily declaring, "It might pay you to remember I'm sheriff of this bailiwick—"

"I'm glad someone finds it a source of satisfaction. Now if you'll turn loose of my arm I've got some chores I'd better tend to."

Butterfly, glaring, licked his lips and said stubbornly, "I want to talk about Geetch—"

"Then you'd better go see him. Geetch and me have parted company."

"Parted . . ." Jones' jaw dropped. "You don't *work* for him anymore?" He peered at her, astounded. "B-but—"

"You're thinking about that race? Geetch won't have any trouble replacing me—he said so himself," she remarked with her lip curled. And, turning her back, she tramped off, leaving Jones standing there.

IX

Jones choused up some pretty devastating replies
but none of these leapt forth until the object of
their venom was safely beyond range. Then he
turned the air pink. This let him breathe a little
freer but produced practically nothing he could ap-
ply to his problems.

Thinking a drink might help he scuffed along to
the Purple Cow and was well into his fourth when
he chanced, in the back bar mirror, to spot Gattison. Throwing down some change Butterfly
caught up his bottle and, picking a somewhat pre-
carious way through the confusion of shifting traffic, dropped into a chair at the little man's table.

The printer, looking put upon, folded both
hands across the top of his glass. "Hi, there," Jones
said as to an old buddy. Gattison's reply was an
unintelligible grunt, but the sheriff did not let this

dampen his grin. He took a pull from his bottle and leaned forward confidentally. "Been aimin' t' look you up, old man. You figured out yet who it was wrecked your plant?"

Eyes darting, the printer mopped at his cheeks, seeming powerfully uncomfortable. A wriggly worm of a man with a scrubby growth across his upper lip and a gray-streaked mane lankly curled about his celluloid collar, the proprietor of Tiedown's now-defunct newspaper looked like something dug out of Skid Row. His bloodshot glance couldn't seem to focus and he squirmed like there were ants in his pants when Jones, setting the bottle off to one side, bent closer to say, "A total loss, was it?"

The man bobbed his head.

"Couldn't save a thing?"

"Well . . ." Gattison said, "I managed to gather up most of the type, but that's about the size of it. No good to me with the press the way it is."

"Couldn't it mebbe be fixed?"

"Those bastards used a sledge! Nothing left of it but junk."

Jones clucked like it had been his own, then said cold as a well chain: "So them broadsheets you got out for Hollister Grisswell was printed some while ago. Ain't that right?"

Gattison stared like a frightened mouse.

"Before, in fact, your place was wrecked. Before any race was ever patched up."

It gave a man something to think about. Jones

thought about it all the way back to the office. It was pretty unnerving to discover such slyness in a man of Grisswell's wealth and standing, in the father of Cathie, the girl of Jones' dreams. Made a man kind of wonder if there was anything left you *could* tie to.

Dudes, of course, by and large were no more reliable than a woman's watch, but it did seem like, being Cathie's old man, it was pretty underhanded to get that kind of thing printed up and plastered all over before Geetch Spangler even knew there was going to *be* any race. It poked up in Jones' mind a batch of pretty ugly notions.

He found Terrazas, back at the office, about ready to shove off for supper. Allowing it would keep another few minutes, Jones waved the coroner back to his chair. He then went over the talk he'd had with Gattison. "Them handbills was readied, right down to the actual terms of the races, before Spangler that day was bamboozled into it. I tell you, by grab, I don't like the smell of it; the dang things was up before I got back t' town!"

"It does look a little peculiar," Terrazas nodded, "but it don't break any laws that I ever heard of."

"But how," Jones glared, "could he be so damn confident?"

"Maybe he knows more about Geetch's horse than Geetch does."

"He don't even know which horse he's gonna run!"

"Well . . . I wouldn't bet on that—"

"I was there," Jones growled. "I heard the whole

thing. Geetch wanted t' know which horse was to be run an' Grisswell, laughin' told him to pick his best. No horse was named except this thoroughbred the dude calls Jubal Jo. So how *could* he know?"

"Probably knows his own horse."

Jones said, snorting: "You ever heard of a thoroughbred beatin' a cow horse in a quarter-mile go? Try usin' what few brains the Lord has given you!"

Terrazas shrugged. Then blew out his cheeks. "There's always a first time," he said, getting up.

Jones scrubbed a hand across raspy jowls. "I just can't figure that feller. This whole business stinks, an' it's gonna git worse. Top of everythin' else that dang female has quit—Mullins I'm talkin' about! She—"

"I know." Terrazas nodded. He said, fishy-eyed, "She's hired on with the dude, and I wish that was all, but you better catch hold of something. Sig Raumeller's in town."

Jones couldn't seem to believe his own ears. "You . . . you mean that gun-fightin' son of a bitch that . . . Hell, you go t' be wrong! Even a knothead like Geetch—"

"It was Sig, all right. I watched him get off the stage, saddle guns and batwing chaps."

"Where is he now?"

"Quien sabe?" the coroner sighed. "Last look I had he was headed for the livery."

Jones, spinning round, grayly peered at the screen.

Terrazas said nervously, "I better go eat."

The old hostler at the livery went on with his chores like both of his ears was stuffed full of cotton. Jones' face darkened angrily but he bit back on his temper long enough to be sure the danged old coot had no intention of answering. Then, reaching out, he took hold of him. "I wasn't just talkin' t' find out if I could! When a stranger rents a horse—"

"Didn't rent 'im, he bought 'im."

"He must've asked how—"

"Never ast nothin'. Just paid me an' left." The old man said sullenly, "That's a arm you got hold of—"

"Never mind that," Jones growled, letting go. "Which way was he pointed?"

"With a thousand an' one things t' do around here—? All right, all *right!*" the hostler cried, backing off. "He took the road t' Gourd an' Vine."

X

Jones looked sick. He felt sick, too. All the fears he'd stood off were back, flapping like buzzards round a broken-legged calf.

That goddam Geetch!

Jones fetched out his horse and flung his rig on, swearing bitterly. Wasn't much chance he would get there in time but, as sheriff, he had to try.

All his life Geetch had run roughshod over others, flattening out anything that got in his way. Acting, by grab, like nobody else had any rights at all! Shooting their cows, trampling their crops, burning—even *killing*, when some damn fool was crazy enough to stand up to him. But Jones had never before heard of Spangler fetching in guns from outside to get a job done. Had the crotchety old bastard finally gone off his rocker?

For the first couple miles Jones applied the steel

freely, not taking any time out to wonder what might happen if he did catch up with this two-handed cannonball. When abruptly he eased off it was mostly, he reminded himself, to make sure he wasn't stranded with a give-out bronc.

Some time could be cut off the trip by short-cutting through a prairie-dog town, taking to the brush and kind of nursing the nag along. And Jones thought about this, giving it the best of what attention he could spare during the next several minutes, adding up the pros and cons.

It was getting dark fast and if he stuck to the road there was no guarantee he wouldn't pass the gink up anyhow. Old Sig wasn't the sort to be snuck up on or be took unawares. Killing was his business and he hadn't got where he was with that game taking unnecessary chances.

In a film of cold sweat it came over Price Jones the smartest thing he could do was cut loose of this dido and dig for the tules. A man could get himself croaked mighty quick scissorsbillin' around with the likes of this Raumeller. Where Butterfly sat in the cold ache of that saddle, the prospect of finding himself a dead hero looked anything but inviting.

Nothing he could chouse up to counteract this appeared to have more weight than a gnat's left eyebrow till he banged head-on into the imagined look of Grisswell's Cathie. This wrung a groan from lips that felt considerable drier than a humped-up bale of Confederate cotton. He couldn't haul off and let Geetch's exterminator make a orphan of her. Now, *could* he?

The answer to that did not require much re-
search. He could see plain as paint no man who
had red blood in his veins could ride off and leave
to fend for herself any girl as sweet as the called-up
visions he found fluttering through his mind.

Just the same he rode on, letting the horse pick
its gait for maybe another ten minutes while he
stood off the reproaches of an over-anxious conscience from unhappily taking to the brush. A man
can shut ears and eyes to a great many things, but
an overactive sense of guilt can sure play hob with
even a guy like Butterfly Jones, old enough to
know better. With a snort of disgust he kicked his
mount into a lope, morbidly wondering if Cathie
would afterwards still care enough to occasionally,
in passing, drop a flower on his grave.

It was close to nine when he raised the ranch's
lights. Unlike the rest of the spreads in this god-
forsaken country, Grisswell's place didn't have to
depend on the sort of coal-oil contraptions other
folks put up with. He had his place electrified by
something that was called a "generator" and had
wires run all over, to the astonishment of all who
saw them. Breasting the last rise Jones found more
lights showing than a man could shake a stick at.

His hopes for this trek skidded down a long
spiral, while his belly's empty hollow took on the
feel of frogs' legs. That night Grisswell's buggy
boss had got him out here before, the only lights
showing had been in the owner's quarters. Even the
bunkhouse was lit up now. He had a darkly nasty
hunch Geetch's gunslinger had got here first.

Got here and gone, he reckoned, deeply sighing. Guessed he might as well ride on in and get it over. Cathie, he opined, was going to take this pretty hard. Whole place, probably, was in a state of shock.

It wasn't until he turned into the yard that the thought came to Jones someone might take a shot at him. Worked up like they'd be over a thing like this—boss cut down right under their noses—this bunch could be jumpy as a boxful of crickets.

He had his mouth half opened when the rove of his glance chanced to pick out at the porch's darkest end a deeper huddle of shadows behind the wink of a spark. Stiffening, staring, he choked off the shout, knees anchoring his horse while he tried to find sense in what he figured to be looking at. Two jaspers sitting there, one of them puffing a quirley or cheroot.

At a time like this.

Smoking, by God!

Seemed pretty near sacrilege the way Jones saw it, trying to rub gooseflesh off the back of his neck. With his eyes like glass chips he took his clamp off the horse and, dropping a hand by the butt of his six-shooter, reined the animal toward them. "Sheriff Jones, here," he called. "You folks havin' trouble?"

"Trouble?" One of that pair on the porch thinly laughed. "Not that we know about. Step down and rest your saddle."

Jones peered harder, about as mixed up now as a feller could get. He felt like a fool. Swearing under his breath he said, "That you, Mister Grisswell?"

"Sounds like you weren't expecting to see me—"

"Who's that up there with you?"

"Come up," Grisswell said. "Like to make you acquainted with the new Gourd and Vine foreman."

XI

Jones, off his horse, stood at the porch's edge, hanging onto his reins and peering at the most notorious notch cutter still making widows in what had been described as "74,000 square miles of pure hell." He was aghast—plumb speechless, at Grisswell's brazen effrontery.

Bad enough, in all conscience, to employ a gink of Sig's stamp in whatever capacity. He found it indescribably worse to think that an owner of Mr. G's educational advantages and commercial accomplishments, *with both eyes open,* could deliberately import and place a cold-blooded killer in a position of authority with so much evident satisfaction.

Jones would sooner have grasped the clawed paw of a hydrophoby skunk than reach out his hand to a pistolero of this stripe—not that

Raumeller made any move. The man's bleached stare was no more readable than a snake's, nor did he bother to get up.

Jones, fiddling with his reins while trying to find enough spit to talk with, finally said too loud, "I'd kind of like—if it wouldn't be no great bother—to git me a look at that Jubal Jo horse you're settin' such store by."

"Certainly," Grisswell said, raising up into the light from the windows to pitch his smoke out into the yard. "No bother to me. You want Shores to go with you?"

"Wouldn't want him t' have to hitch up jest fer that. I can find my way, I reckon."

And he set off with a wave, glad to get clear of that pet cobra's stare, but somewhat worried, too, by the bland mocking texture of Grisswell's smile.

He let go of his reins outside the stables, leaving his horse while he went up the runway, finding the place bright as daylight. Horses looked inquisitively around from their stalls, a couple softly whinnying, one pampered bay impatiently pawing a hole the way some running horses will. At the end of the line he found a gray stallion, but the name card tacked beside the Dutch door said *Telachapi Tom*. Nowhere did Butterfly see the black he hunted.

Then he found, somewhat surprised, a door he'd supposed would lead to the clutter of pens out back actually opened into an ell and another double line of stalls, presently dark. Feeling around for a switch he pushed this door open wider. Deep in that darkness he caught a flutter of movement,

77

more heard than glimpsed. Before he could swallow, the place was flooded with light and he found himself gaping at a gimlet-eyed jasper crouched over the gleam of a murderous two-barreled sawed-off shotgun. With twin rasping clicks both hammers went back.

"Hey!" Jones gasped. "Watch out fer that thing! You wanta *kill* somebody?"

"Wotcher doin' back 'ere?"

"Lookin' fer that horse—"

"Wot I figgered!"

Jones didn't care for the tone of that at all. "Now see here," he cried, "I got a perfect right—" and stopped, jerking round as someone came up beside him. "Cripes, am I glad t' see *you!*" he exclaimed. "Tell that feller, Rockabye . . ."

The look she gave him would have turned off a tap. "What *are* you doing here?"

She looked pretty grim.

"Well, hell's fire! Dang it, I'm sheriff an'—"

"I expect that's one fact we can't get around." Then she said, "As such you should know this table's private property."

"Well, sure. Of course it is. Belongs to Mr. Grisswell. He knows I'm here. Told me himself I could . . ."

"All right, Jeeter. You can put up the gun," Charlie Mullins said, and, to Jones: "After what happened to that pony horse of Geetch's you can understand why we've got to take precautions. We got that race coming up. If anything happened to keep Jubal out of it Mr. Grisswell stands to lose ten thousand dollars."

It was as near, Jones guessed, as she could come to an apology. It scarcely made up for the fright he'd been given and did even less toward bolstering his hurt dignity. Still smarting he growled, "I don't have t' be hit over the head to know when I ain't wanted!"

The guy with the double-barreled made a rude noise. With her mousy hair in that untidy bun, the girl lifted her chin to eye Jones' riled face. "Sometimes," she said, "I get to wonderin' about you," and left it lay there between them like a pan of sour dough.

Jones, cheeks darkening, spun to paw for the door. "Hell, don't go away mad," sniggered the clown with the shotgun; and Jones swung back, anger in every outraged line of him.

The Mullins female said with a kind of startled haste, "Come on—I'll give you a knockdown to Jubal," and set off past Jeeter toward the corridor's far end.

Jones, half minded to refuse, scowlingly followed.

By the rear wall she stopped to face the left-hand stall. "There. What do you think of him?"

An arched head came over the door but Butterfly hardly glanced at the horse. Eyes widening the girl nervously poked at her hair. "Was it Jubal you came here to see or *me?*"

"I'd like t' know why you run out on Geetch. . . ."

"That's flattering, I must say. Sometimes, Butterfly—"

"My name's Price, an' I'm not so damn stupid as

some people think! Your boss an' Geetch could save a powerful lot of trouble if they'd call off this race."

She peered at him astonished. "You out of your mind?"

"Can't you *see* it? First one thing, then it's half a dozen others, all of 'em calculated t' kick up a feud." He said, softly earnest: "Think back a bit. Charlie. Somebody's *usin'* them two."

For a moment, wide-eyed, she considered him intently, then scorn closed him out. With a sniff she said tartly, "That star's gone to your head."

For a moment it seemed Jones was minded to argue. Then, clamping his jaws, he swung around and tramped off.

Outside, by his horse, he scrubbed a hand across hot cheeks. Snapping up the reins he climbed into the saddle. Without bothering to speak to the pair on the porch he put his horse down the lane, half-way minded to ride on over to Spangler's and see if he couldn't talk some sense into Geetch.

Wrapped in the churn of tumultuous thoughts, at first he didn't notice the shape by the gate, not even when he bent to open the barrier. The first hint he had that he was not alone came with the faint but heady fragrance of crushed violets. Then he saw her standing in the shadows of twin poplars.

He felt a great upsurge of relief. *She* would understand. Her mind wasn't closed against new thoughts like Charlie Mullins', or stunted by pride and intolerance like Spangler's. And she was young enough to listen and weigh a sheriff's words. She had her father's ear. If anyone could help get this stopped it was Cathie.

With so much assurance flowing through his veins, Jones said, "Look—you've got to git your ol' man t' call this race off! An' the quicker the better. This—"

She said: "I couldn't do that." Then, seeing him stiffen, she adopted a more reasonable tone, saying, like Eve giving the nudge to the serpent, "If you think it's the thing to do, I'll talk to him, of course. But you have to realize Daddy has his heart set on this. Ever since we came here people have been telling him what wonderfully fast horses Mr. Spangler has, and how preposterous it is to imagine *any*thing could beat them, least of all a thoroughbred. Why, you'd think to hear them talk that Jubal was some animated freak, fit only to stand at the end of a leadshank.

"Daddy wants people to like him, but he's determined to show them how wrong they are. Jubal was *bred* in speed. For more than five generations all his forebears were celebrated racehorses. His sire is Plaudit, who won the Kentucky Derby. His dam was Cinderella. She has produced more great track performance horses than any mare now alive. And Plaudit's father was one of the greatest speed horses in the history of the turf! Why—"

"Maybe so," Jones broke in, "but the big problem here, far as I'm concerned, ain't got nothin' t' do with who gits beat. It's the hurt feelin's an' hate that race'll work up, an' what it'll do to the country if this outfit an' Spangler's decide t' settle things with guns. You better pass on the word; an' if he figures t' stay healthy the very least he kin do is git rid of that gunny—"

"Gunny!" she said with her eyes big and round.

"That new range boss he's hired. That Sig Raumeller jigger . . ."

Even in the uncertain light of these stars Jones glimpsed the startled change in her expression. She seemed to kind of draw back, one hand coming up, while her eyes—great black pearls—swept his face with a dreadful astonishment.

"He'd never do that. You must have rocks in your head."

"But Cathie—the guy's a notch-cuttin' killer!"

"Of course he is. Daddy's no fool!" she cried in a surge of rebellious impatience. "Did you imagine we'd sit here and twiddle our fingers while Geetch Spangler takes this place away from us? The Grisswells have dealt with pirates before!"

XII

Jones went to bed that night with his clothes on. Not expecting to sleep, he lay like a rock, completely out of this world until he woke, half fried with the sun in his face, to find the morning about gone.

Peering blearily, he knuckled stuck-together lids and pushed up, morosely scowling through a series of yawns till his glance chanced to brighten on a near-emptied bottle. Worrying the cork from its neck he held it up to the light and, shuddering, swallowed, belching noisily as he put the thing down.

He finally got up, feeling somewhat more able in a creaky sort of way. Harold Terrazas came through the drag of the screen as he was scraping the last of the soap off his cheeks. "Salud!" the coroner said and grinned sardonically. "I see you got back more or less in one piece."

Jones, dabbing a nick at the side of his jaw, grunted.

"I guess," Terrazas cocked his head, "you must have found Geetch in a down mood for sure, real tore up at being caught in such a caper. Otherwise—"

"I didn't see Geetch. Raumeller," Jones growled, swinging around, "took the road t' Gourd an' Vine."

"That figures. Not much point riding out to see Spangler till he'd earned whatever they settled on. Reckon Geetch'll try to hand him some of that paper?"

Butterfly said fiercely, "This ain't no time for jokes. By grab! When I think of all the ridin' I done tryin' t' save that peckerneck from bein' blown t' dollrags— You know what the dude has done? Made Sig his range boss! Can you beat that fer stupid?"

"He tell you that?"

"Cathie claims 'Daddy' hired him as a kind of insurance!" Jones said, disgusted, "I'd as soon have a goddam rattlesnake around!"

"You tell Grisswell that?"

"I didn't tell him nothin'. Didn't have no chance to with Raumeller settin' right there on the porch. . . . I took a look at that horse though. An' that Mullins is pretty near loco as Grisswell. Acts like she figures they got a real chance t' win!"

Terrazas, rubbing his jaw, eyed Jones thoughtfully. "I've a halfway notion to drop a few bucks, you got any spare cash?"

"I sure ain't got none to throw away!"

"Last odds quoted was thirty to one. Man could get well fast with a hundred at that price." He flopped down in the swivel and hung his boots on Jones' desk. "You got to hand it to Geetch, putting that pistolman on Gourd and Vine as range boss. Looks like there's a bite in the old wolf yet."

Jones peered sharply. "You don't really think he done that, do you?"

The coroner shrugged. "It's something to consider. Look back at what's happened since you got sworn in. Three hombres stick up the Purple Cow. Ferguson, loaded, gets his light blown out. Both those crimes had a basis in money, and who's short of coin? Plenty of fellows maybe, but Spangler has to be pretty near desperate."

He took down his feet, swiveled up to the desk, got out his pad and picked up a pencil. Jones shook his head. "We don't know that, Harold. And you're forgettin' Gattison."

"We don't even know that Gattison comes into it. Common denominator seems to be money. No money changed hands when that print shop was wrecked. Grudge, maybe. We know Geetch is short. Been paying his hands with I.O.U.'s; saloons have chopped off his credit. Six of his punchers, packing their plunder, took the stage out of here for greener pastures. He's been cock of the walk around Tiedown for years, the Number One Mogul . . . Mister Big himself. What's happened to his wealth? And if he's really in a bind howcome he doesn't step around to the bank?"

"He made his pile in cattle," Jones growled. "We've had three years of drought. It's hit all them ranchers, an' Geetch was overstocked. Why, if it wasn't fer the Verdigris River runnin' . . . this whole damn country's about t' blow away! Forced sales have dropped prices—cattle right now is a drag on the market."

Terrazas made some more marks with the pencil. "*His* kind of cattle. Gourd and Vine's got no trouble."

"Whitefaces!" Jones sneered. "Pedigreed stuff raised with kid gloves inside fenced pastures on irrigated grass! Rich man's toys!"

"Takes money," Terrazas nodded. "But the writing's on the wall. They'll all have to come to it—"

"Not Geetch!" Jones said fiercely.

The coroner, smiling, made a couple of squiggles on the pad with his pencil and looked up at Jones blandly. "'That's right. Too set in his ways. Too pinched in the cash box. But he's got to do something or go under; in his bust-a-gut way he must have seen this himself. Tries a flyer in horses, finds his luck is still bad. Gets whipped where it hurts. About then, like as not, he's faced with neck meat or nothing.

"He scrapes the bottom of the barrel, groaning up the price to buy the hides that foxed him, and they're good. He wins a few, but the word gets around. They're all talking now about Geetch Spangler's racers. He's had it. Nobody round here will take a run at him."

"There's other places."

Terrazas nodded. "But now he's down to pretty much working with paper. He had a deal on with Rockabye to take Curtain Raiser and that gray, Eight Below, over into Texas where he stood some chance to get well, but that girl's pretty cagey. With the deal still in the dickering stage Grisswell throws that Fair race at him and, quick as he's hooked, hires his trainer away from him.

"Put yourself in Geetch's place. More hay than he can spare and all the best of his range—those Hat Creek sections have been dumped in with the hope of making that dude look like a busted flush. With Mullins he might have done it. But he hasn't got Mullins anymore; the dude's got her."

Jones pawed at his face. Aggravated and scowling he settled his butt against the edge of the desk. "How'd you know he had a deal on with Charlie t' go over into Texas?"

"One thing us Mexicans around here has got is cousins. Happens one of mine is still on Geetch's payroll—Charco Tavares."

Jones' stare was suspicious. "Even so," he finally grumbled, "I can't see where that ties him to this gunhawk."

"Did you know that dude's been buying up Geetch's paper?"

"Where'd you git that?"

"I got to thinking," Terrazas said, "it might give us a line to know how bad Geetch was hurting. So I checked up a little. The Purple Cow, before they shut off his credit, was holding Spangler notes to-

taling three hundred dollars. He was into the Aces
Up for five hundred and ten. Grisswell's buggy
boss latched onto both sets. I went over to the
Mercantile. Wilson admits Geetch was into him for
plenty. He wouldn't say how much but—"

"Did he sell Geetch's paper to Shores?"

"Sold it to someone, and at a pretty good profit
from the look in his eye. I found out something
else. Shores was in town the day those cowpokes
took off. Geetch's debts that I've pinned down will
run at close to three thousand. Right now you
couldn't—"

"If it's Grisswell—"

"It's not Shores. The fellow hasn't got that kind
of dough."

Jones, stewing, fumed. "Why would that
dude . . . ?"

"He never done it for love."

"But you much as just said *Geetch* was the one
put Raumeller over there! I'm so tangled up
now—"

"It's kind of tricky," Terrazas nodded, "but who
else would profit from having Grisswell killed? It's
Spangler that's hurting. Surely you can see that?
And the dude's been rubbing salt in his wounds.
He's built up a show place right under Geetch's
nose; sets him off for the ignorant brush-popper he
is. Then he hooks Geetch into this big-stakes race,
piles insult on injury by walking off with Geetch's
trainer—and don't forget Spangler thinks the dude
is responsible for the loss of that pony horse, that
Papago Pete some joker run off with. And now this

blamed dude is buying up Geetch's notes. Don't it seem like to you a man in Geetch's fix would get to thinking all his troubles could be laid at Grisswell's door?''

Jones looked worried, no two ways about it.

Terrazas said, getting up, "You've got to see Spangler the way he's been all his life, bellicose and grabby; and the way he sees himself, cow-baron boss of this whole scabby county ... a top dog being hamstrung by a dude.''

XIII

Put that way it did not seem unreasonable to see Raumeller in the cushy saddle of being able to draw pay from two owners simultaneously. So long, anyway, as he could manage to hold off from killing the goose.

Though Terrazas' notions nagged him considerably, Jones wasn't satisfied that such was the case. He couldn't see how Geetch, with that bully-puss temper, could have found enough patience—not to mention savvy—to have planted the man so cleverly on Grisswell. And the dude *had* fetched the leather slapper into this. *Did you imagine,* Cathie had cried, *we'd sit here and twiddle our fingers while Geetch Spangler takes this place away from us!*

Trying to worry some sense from it, Jones had no idea when Terrazas departed; when he glanced around the coroner was gone. Despite the case the man had built against Geetch it seemed to Jones more likely that both these moguls were considerably at fault, each of them apparently thinking the other was trying to put him out of business. If the dude, as claimed by Terrazas, had been buying Geetch's notes, it was probably no more than as something—like Raumeller—he had done in the hope of keeping Spangler in line.

Jones was not, however, encouraged by this to relax in the view that it would all blow away. He was uncomfortably aware how little was needed to nudge this pair into a full-scale feud. He still believed someone else to be back of it, someone maneuvering these moguls to reap personal gain and either pick up the pieces or advantage himself in some other fashion, under cover of the smoke once the guns got to banging.

It was not a pleasant prospect for a man to take to breakfast, and Jones, distractedly reminded of his empty belly, abruptly scooped up his hat with a snort of disgust.

His glance fell across the pad on which Terrazas had doodled. Almost against his will something about the penciled scratchings pulled him closer, and he bent over to stare at the pictured likeness of Spangler's face. All the man's worst qualities had been cunningly captured and frozen into an expression of vindictive hate.

The sheriff, shaken, tore off the sheet and shoved it, grumbling, into his pocket. But the naked savagery of it stayed in his mind to needle him all the way to the restaurant. Was Terrazas right? Was it Geetch's bitter rage that was fomenting all this discord?

If not Geetch, who then? Flancher? Bernagrowt? Eph Wilson, the storekeeper? None of these had the brains or the heft to spur ambition. It was hard to see how any one of them could profit from the turmoil of a range war. A banker might, but Jones could not see Ed Gretchen in the part. The man was too prissy, too chintzy and close, to risk what he had in such an out-and-out gamble. It took a bolder spirit and one twisted by something sharper than cupidity. He was a man more apt to despise than hate.

Gretchen might resent Grisswell, but Spangler's account had nursed him along when no comparable assets had been even in sight. He might refuse Geetch credit in a time tough as this, but Jones couldn't see him engineering Geetch's downfall.

Having padded his ribs the sheriff of Tiedown tramped morosely around to the Purple Cow. The place was being swamped out but he found the owner, O'Halleran, working over his accounts. The Irishman looked up without his usual twinkle. "An' fer what would you be comin' around at this ungodly hour? A nip at the dog that bit ye?"

"Might not be a bad idea," Jones scowled, "but as a matter of fact I'm here on business—"

"No business of mine, I can be sure of that. Go on. Git yer drink an' be off."

A bunching of muscles bulged the sheriff's jaw. "This is *law* business, Eddie—"

"So? Ye've caught them spalpeens that stuck me place up three—"

"Well, no . . . not exactly . . ."

"Didn't figure ye had." The Irishman snorted. "I'll be money ahead to write it off an' fergit it if I got t' depend on the likes of you."

With a hard, scornful glare he was about to get back to work on his books when Butterfly said on a defensive impulse, "I'll make it up to you—"

"I should live so long?" The Irishman, sighing, said, "Spare me the fairy tales. Just say what ye've come fer an' git on with it, lad."

"That big winnin' of Ferguson's . . . I understand Spangler was one of the big losers. Didn't I hear he was short of cash?"

The saloon keeper chewed his lip for a moment. "I wasn't playin' that night but I was there; the game had already started when Geetch dropped in. Had a roll in his mitt that would choke a giraffe. One twenty folded round a bunch of ones, twos an' fives." O'Halleran sniffed. "The boys weren't too happy an' got some agg'avated when Mahls took the wad an' set ten blues in front av him. You could tell Geetch was hungry. There was a slug of paper in that game when they finished."

"How much'd he stick you for?"

A kind of sour smile walked across the man's mouth. "Didn't take me fer any that night—nor Mahls. Jack had already told him he was through playin' bank before Shores got into us. All I had was six months of his bar chits."

"Five hundred an' ten bucks worth? He swill that much likker in—?"

"Him an' his hands." O'Halleran nodded.

"They been drinkin' like fish. How'd . . . Terrazas told you, eh?"

"How much of Geetch's paper did that leaser go off with?"

"Fifteen hundred . . . coupla thousan' mebbe."

Jones stared at his thoughts. "Well, thanks," he said. "I'll see if I can't git a lead on them stickups."

"Don't strain yerself, boy," O'Halleran said, and Jones flushed.

Back in the sun he mulled it over some more. Thing had more angles than a dog has fleas. Had the stickup at O'Halleran's been part of the whole, or just an isolated incident like the sledgehammer smashing of Gattison's press? Could a man even be sure that that had no connection with the animosity stirred up between Geetch and Grisswell?

Terrazas had dismissed it as the work of a crank. But Gattison had held Geetch up to censure before. When the Twiddler family had been run off their place the paper had carried a bristling editorial, asking how long would people stand for Spangler's bullying. Been no love lost between them two. And busting up that press had been just the kind of stunt a man would look for Geetch to pull.

With such an influx of strangers in town for the Fair, as sheriff, Price Jones felt it incumbent to keep himself in circulation. The county's annual wingding was due officially to open this evening at six with a display of baked tasties, patchwork quilts, hooked rugs, rag rugs, fudges and taffies, leather goods and whatnot. Tomorrow's schedule included bronc riding, bull riding, wild-cow milking and roping, plus three matched races—in addition to the much publicized quarter-mile dash between Geetch and the dude.

Terrazas was also policing the crowds. Jones saw him several times during the course of the afternoon, though never near enough to speak with. There were a lot of hard faces moving through the jostling throngs. Twice he had to break up fights. At five-thirty, feeling like something dragged through a knothole, he went round again to the Lone Star—Grub, and climbing onto a stool at the oilcloth-covered counter, proceeded through habit to feed his face.

At six, he was irritably back on the street and, at six-fifteen, gravitating toward the livery where, to ease aching feet, he picked up his horse. He could not shut off the worrisome thoughts that hung in his mind like a clutch of bats. He could feel the tension the way a patched bone feels the approach of a storm. Its brittle grip was in the pinched shine of faces, the too boisterous laughter. Had Spangler, desperate, killed that leaser for the poker winnings that had bulged the man's pockets? Did anyone besides Terrazas suspect him?

Where else could he have got hold of the cash he had bet on the outcome of tomorrow's race? From the bank? On a mortgage perhaps? Was he one of the three who'd stuck up the Purple Cow? Was the theft of that pony horse really a felony or just something cooked up to give him an excuse to tie into Grisswell?

Questions. Questions. They were thicker than coyotes around a lost lamb! How else could Geetch have gotten the money, though? During the afternoon, checking both saloons, Jones had made it his business to look into that betting. Spangler, covering odds against his horse Eight Below, had put up with the barkeeps—in hard coin of the realm—more than twenty-two hundred dollars!

Most of the jostling throngs had by this time begun to drift in the direction of the stockyards, where, in the big auction barn built of corrugated tin, the competition in exhibits had been set up for display so that folks would be able to watch the judging. Jones reckoned he had better perambulate over there.

He would liked to have been able to sit down with Geetch and thrash out some of these things he found so uncomfortable to contemplate. But a man could just as well talk to a rock as expect to get any change out of Spangler. It had become one of the established facts of life around here that in his cattle-baron role Geetch did the asking. He was above giving answers.

Jones shook his head. When Geetch came up against something a glare couldn't whip, his likeliest reaction was to reach for a gun.

Riding his horse about the fringes of the crowd for a while, listening to the snatches of talk and keeping both eyes peeled to spot and stop trouble before it could get out of hand, an hour or so later Jones found himself staring at Geetch.

The rancher had two of his hands in tow, both

hard specimens, standing back and watching the yokels with that sour tolerance which had become so much a part of him. It was the first time the sheriff had caught a look at the man since that day at Gourd & Vine when, at Trimbo's insistance, he'd gone out there over the matter of Geetch's missing pony horse and wound up accepting Cathie's invite to lunch.

It wasn't at all likely the old man had forgotten. Or forgiven it, either. In Spangler's book Jones' refusal to ride off with him had gone down either as rebellion or the whim of a stupid fool. A black mark, for there were no shades of gray in the cattle king's judgment of other folks' motives. You either walked where Geetch said or prepared for the consequences.

Considering this, Butterfly regarded the thought of confronting him with something less than outright enthusiasm. It just didn't seem like the right time to do it. Geetch's normally ruddy face seemed more than usually belligerent, and there was a bitterness in him—a kind of barren coarseness seeping through the hard twisted cast of his features that was visible even from here.

Jones, dryly swallowing, excused himself on the grounds that really there was nothing he could say. There was no evidence against the man, nothing that would stand up in a court of law. If Terrazas' contentions had any basis at all, or Cathie's voiced suspicion, the most obvious start for uncovering Geetch's guilt might well lie in the whereabouts of that allegedly missing pony horse.

Jones wondered why he hadn't happened onto this notion before.

But where would a man start looking?

If the horse hadn't been stolen it seemed a pretty good bet the animal probably had been penned up someplace inside the confines of Spangler's ranch. And, in that case, it seemed to Jones, the coroner's cousin, Charco Tavares, would be the man to get in touch with. And right now, by grab, while Geetch was here in town, looked the best time to take a stab at it.

Unaware that the rancher had observed his prolonged scrutiny, Jones, still thinking about Tavares and the missing Papago Pete, reined his mount away from the barn and jogged off uptown on a hunt for Terrazas.

He went first to the two saloons and, not finding him there, cut back toward the combination office and jail. Dusk was beginning to darken the view and several shopkeepers had got their lamps lit in the hope of enticing into their tills some of the out-of-town dollars still restively tramping the warped plank walks.

The office was filled with thickening shadows. Even so Butterfly put his head round the screen before he would believe the coroner wasn't there. It was much too late for him to have gone home for supper. He wasn't on the street and, after watching awhile, it seemed equally unlikely the man would be found in one of the stores.

Tempted to give it up, the sheriff considered the street once more. He didn't want to jeopardize the project by leaving a note which anyone who happened into the office might read. So far as was known the man was happily married, but Jones, ever a lukewarm believer in the theory of wedded bliss, on a sudden hunch climbed back in the saddle and kneed his horse toward the south end of town.

A well-beaten path led off through the brush that concealed Tiedown's shame. There, behind closed shutters in an unpainted cluster of whoppy-jawed shacks, the madams conducted their clandestine business. But though he knocked at every door no one admitted having seen Terrazas and, disgruntled, Jones reckoned any hands left at the ranch would be in bed time he got there.

Angling back toward the stockyards in this uncertain light he was rounding the rear of Berna-growt's saddle shop when something whipped past his ear with the whine of a hornet. In that split second of frozen astonishment—even before he could reach up to cuff at it—a gun's flat crack viciously broke from the alley.

Jones, yelling, raked the horse with his spurs and, flattening himself as much as he could, drove his mount full tilt into the first hole available. This was the slot between the Dutchman's west wall and the adjacent Lone Star Grub.

Careening into the street, pistol naked and lifted, the first thing Jones saw in the light from the storefronts was the barrel-chested shape and startled face of Spangler's range boss.

XIV

Trimbo did not have the street to himself. There were other dark shapes stiffly caught in Jones' stare, fixed as the figures in a wax museum—even a fringe-topped surrey behind matched bays, eyes rolling with fright, in the brittle hush; but it was Spangler's man who drew and held the sheriff's attention.

The matched pair moved. The spell was broken as additional people, some running, most of them avidly gaping, converged on the scene with a clatter of questions inspired by thrill-hungry, morbid curiosity.

Neither Trimbo nor Jones gave them any kind of notice.

Jones made no move to get out of the saddle. In headlong anger he furiously cried: "You throw that shot at me?"

Trimbo shook his head like a man confused. His tongue licked out and crossed parched lips. He swallowed a couple of times and said in the voice of a man shook from sleep, "I'm right where I was when the sound of it stopped me—"

"All who believe that kin stand on their heads!"

"Man it's the *truth*. Take a look at my gun—"

"You snake-eyed son of a bitch," Jones snarled, "the truth ain't in you!"

Trimbo took it in silence. They could all see Jones was aching to shoot. Spangler's man hoarsely said, "If you'd look at my gun . . ."

Some measure of caution must have seeped through Jones' rage. Still reared in the stirrups like a scorpion with its tail up, he said more reasonably: "All right. Pass it over."

Trimbo drew a full breath. Approaching in the manner of a wet-footed cat, the Quarter Circle S ramrod gingerly drew the pistol from its anchorage in his belt and, grasping the weapon by its barrel with his left hand, stopped beside the shoulder of Jones' mount to hand it up.

Butterfly lifted the muzzle and grimly sniffed. It was plain the Colt had not recently been fired, but this didn't mean the range boss did not have another smaller weapon concealed about him somewhere.

With his own .44 tucked under his arm Jones broke open Trimbo's pistol, shook out the loads and dropped them in his pocket. Knowing he could not search the man here without piling up risks he didn't have to take, he tossed the empty weapon

back. With his own gun resettled in his fist he said:
"Expect you better come down to my office."

The man scowled. "What for?"

"We'll look into that more careful when we git
there. Start walkin'."

Something relieved, almost slyly amused, briefly
flickered in Trimbo's considering stare. Then he
shrugged and struck off.

Sitting back in his saddle Jones walked the horse
after him, narrowly watching for tricks. But as he
wheeled past the surrey a glance up the reins sur-
prisedly widened on the face and approving smile
of Cathie Grisswell. Warmed by this he touched his
hat, and, feeling a little foolish about the pistol, put
it away.

He supposed she and her parent had come in to
see the exhibits, though Grisswell himself was not
presently visible. Jones was flattered to think such
important people were not above openly regis-
tering their interest. He knew well enough what a
poor figure he cut in the eyes of these penny-
pinching counter-jumping merchants—you wouldn't
see none of them rushing forward to help him!

He hoped Terrazas would be at the office, but he
wasn't. The place was still dark when Butterfly told
Trimbo to stop by the steps. Swinging down in the
shadows he ducked under the rail, having anchored
the horse, was about to order Spangler's range boss
inside when the he-coon himself stepped out of the
night with a blustery growl, "What the hell's goin'
on here?"

It caught Jones off balance, and while he was

trying to find wind enough to talk with Trimbo said, "It looks like a shakedown—"

"Now wait a minute," Jones snarled. "Some joker took a shot at me out back of Bernagrowt's, an' when I come larrupin' into the street this character was roundin' the front of that shop—"

"Why don't you tell him the truth?" Trimbo jeered. "I was just walkin' past, and I wasn't the only one. There was anyways five or six other guys out there."

Spangler was in a real sod-pawing mood. His back was arched like a mule in a hailstorm and the veins stood out thick as ropes on his neck. But Jones had some spleen of his own to get rid of. "If you was so dadblamed innocent," he cried, "what'd you stop fer when I come outa that alley? Hah? Answer me that! Them others musta thought you'd run into a wall."

"The look of you on that horse, jaws flappin', eyes flamin', was enough to cramp anyone," Trimbo came back. "I thought, by Gawd, you'd gone clean off your rocker."

"Never mind my rock—you just git up them steps," Jones snarled, skinning his teeth, "or I'm liable t' forget what I'm packin' this badge fer!"

While his trouble-shooter hesitated, looking halfway minded to test the sheriff's mettle, Spangler, rearing up, appeared about to flip his lid. "You can't jail a man for starin'!" he shouted. "What the goddam hell're you tryin' to *do* t' me!"

"You better take a look at what you're doin' to yourself," Jones advised, sounding testy. "It won't hurt this feller to spend a night in the jug—"

But the Quarter Circle S owner, waving his arms and half-strangled, yelled: "I ain't thinkin' about *him!* We got a race t' run tomorrer an' a horse t' keep our eyes on, an' after what happened t' Papago Pete—"

"Alls I want," Jones cut in, but Spangler, bellowing like a sore-backed bull, drowned him out. "I don't care about that! *You can't have him now!* Until we're done with that race I want him down at the stockyards—"

"Too bad about you. There's folks is plumb fed up with your wants," Jones grated, too riled to curb the churn of his bile. "All their lives they been jumpin' through hoops for Quarter Circle S, bowin' an' scrapin' like a bunch of goddam monkeys! You ain't God A'mighty, Spangler! Now git the hell away from here before I run you in!"

It looked for a bit as though the rancher would go for his gun. No one before had ever spoke to him so free, and his old man's face took on the kind of splotchy pallor of a gent not two breaths away from having a stroke.

His eyes bulged like squeezed grapes. His mouth worked, and the skin hanging in wrinkles below the jut of his trembling chin lifted and dropped like the wattles of a gobbler, but nothing came out that a man could make any sense of.

Jones, spinning around, gave Trimbo such a shove toward the steps, the man, caught in the lock of his spurs, went down with a thump that shook the whole porch.

You talk about mad!

Trimbo's lips peeled back from his fangs like a snake's. The hiss of his breath was like a snake's too, but the rage-blurred hand making a pass for his belt suddenly stopped in mid-motion when he found himself gaping into the snout of Jones' gun. "Go ahead," Jones drawled—"don't wait on me!"

XV

A sizable crowd half ringed them in. Jones, irritably eyeing the nearer faces, said, "All right, sports, fun's over. Break it up," and watched them draw reluctantly off. A bunch of goddam sheep, he thought, listening to the receding mutter and mumble. Small wonder Spangler took them for fools. Dropping the hip-held .44 into its scuffed holster he took a hard look at Trimbo and shook his head. "You might as well git goin' too."

Shouldering past he went up the steps, yanked open the screen and passed into the gloom of the unlighted office. Still in the clutch of this sour disenchantment he was reaching for the lamp when the tail of his glance picked out the black hulk of a shape against the window.

"For Pete's sake what are *you doin*'?" he growled.

Terrazas, putting the shotgun aside, said on a sigh of let-go breath, "If he'd touched that pistol I was figuring to blast him loose of his britches."

"Trimbo?" Jones, staring, snorted. "Guess you're no brighter than the rest of us yokels. No more harm to that guy than you'd find in a sparrow."

The coroner said anxiously, "You been working too hard?"

Jones found the lamp, scratched a match and got it lit. "I been too close to the woods t' see the kind of timber that's growed up around us."

"What's that supposed to mean?"

"Where the devil have you been? Did you know I looked all over for you?"

"Was afraid you might. I didn't dare leave a note." Terrazas sat tiredly down on the cot. "Let me catch my breath. What's all this about Trimbo?"

"We been diddled," Jones growled. "The guy's a fourteen-carat fake. Looks tough, sounds tough, with no more guts than a sackful of straw. They've took in the whole range with that bleach-eyed bum."

"He didn't look like no bum when he was going for that pistol."

"That's what's made him so important to Geetch. I been as scared of that whippoorwill as any damn kid in three-cornered pants. But never again!" Jones tossed a handful of cartridges onto the desk. "That gun was dehorned an' both of us knowed it."

Terrazas seemed doubtful, and gruffly said, "He's done some pretty rough things for a guy without guts."

"That kinda stuff comes easy when you're holdin' the whip hand."

"Then you think it's all Geetch?"

"I don't know what I think." Jones glared at his fists as though minded to break something. "Where was you when I was combin' this town?"

"Quarter Circle S—probably on the way back. I went out to see Charco." The coroner said, leaning forward: "We found that horse."

"Spangler's lead pony?"

The Mexican nodded. "Dead as hell in the bottom of a gulch. Birds had been at him but it was Pete, all right. . . . You don't look too excited," he said.

"Stood to reason he'd be on Spangler's range someplace. But that don't mean Spangler put 'im there."

"It don't?" Terrazas studied Jones with his head to one side. "What does it take to convince you, man?"

"More'n I've had my nose rubbed in so far."

They stared at each other while the silence piled up and the wind outside pulled groans from the rafters. "Look at it," Jones said. "All of a kind. Everything we turn up seems t' point square at Geetch. Don't that appear kind of strange to you?"

"No," Terrazas said. "Not to me it don't. That old mossyhorn has been boss in these parts since about the year One. Only guy round that don't eat out of his hand is that dude. He don't have to and it's burned Spangler up. He can't abide Grisswell's guts."

"So you figure he took an' killed his own horse to put Grisswell on a limb he could saw cut from under him?" Jones said morosely, "Afraid I can't buy it."

"What you see shaping here doesn't rest on that. Grisswell's maneuvered him into a race, set the conditions himself . . . stakes Geetch would hate to lose. Stakes he can't afford. Then this loco dude hires his trainer away. On top of everything else the man's hard up for cash. Half his crew walks off. Then Grisswell sends Shores around buying up his notes—"

"You make almost as good a case against the dude, and I'd as soon suspect him as this nizzy old fool that's put his back to the wall to buy a bunch of crazy bangtails he's got no goddam use fer." Jones blew out his cheeks in an irritable sigh. "It just goes t' prove what I been sayin' all along. Somebody wants them two t' lock horns an' they're just cross-grained enough t' pitch in an' help."

"All right," Terrazas said. "Who you putting your chips on? Eph Wilson the storekeeper? How'll it help him? The proprietor of Tiedown's plush hotel? Bernagrowt the saddlemaker?"

"There's other people lives around here that could profit."

"I can't think of no one but Gretchen the banker and a range war wouldn't do *him* too much good."

"Oh, I don't know," Jones grumbled. "It would

give him an excuse to pick up some pretty fair spreads for the price of foreclosure."

"You think it's him?" Terrazas looked his astonishment.

"Hell, no. But I could easier think it was him than Geetch. Mebbe I'm stubborn," Jones said grumpily, "but I just can't see a guy out to make trouble leavin' himself as wide open as Geetch is."

"Maybe you ought to look again at his past. You see anything hidden about the way he got his land?"

"He sure never wishy-washied around like this!"

"Probably cramped his style when all them boys quit—"

"I'll tell you one feller could profit. An' he could be sore at both of 'em—Gattison."

They sat a while considering it. "He's a terrier," the coroner, frowning, admitted. "He gets hold of a thing he's hard to shake loose. It could be the reason he got put out of business. . . ."

"But the guy," Jones went on, "puts the goose bumps on me is that damn Sig Raumeller. Deal like this is just made for his kind."

"Which brings us right back to Geetch," Terrazas nodded. "Where there's so much smoke there's got to be some fire, and he's the one guy that's really hurting. He's been hit with more luck, and all of it bad, than the rest of them laid end to end put together. A few fresh stiffs strewed around through the brush wouldn't no more bother him than worms in his biscuits. A shooting war—"

"F' pete's sake, Terrazas, you got Geetch on the brain!"

"Close your eyes if you want to, but facts is facts and you can't get around them," the coroner said doggedly. "There's plenty of evidence—"

"The man is bein' framed."

"You don't believe he's hard up?"

"I never said that."

"Then where'd he get the twenty-two hundred he's put up at the bars to cover that race!"

XVI

Jones tossed and turned half the night until finally, desperate, he got up and hit the bottle. Even that was no better than a temporary crutch. It let him get to sleep but the morning found his problems just as big and black as ever. Considerably blacker, even more pressing, because today was the date of that confounded race. And one thing he'd certainly got to face up to. If Geetch wasn't the skunk hid under this woodpile, they were faced with the necessity of providing an alternative.

He kind of wished now he had let Gretchen sack him.

His legs weren't too steady and his head howled like the inside of a stamp mill as he scooped up his hat and clapped his shell belt around him. All the way to the Lone Star Grub the pound in his head kept banging away at that one stinking word. *Who?*

Who had set this pot boiling? Who, besides Geetch, could look to better his condition by stirring these antagonisms? Who had known enough about either of their wants and needs and personal involvements to prod these two moguls into each thinking the other was out to do him in?

He supposed uneasily it *could* be Gattison, but he didn't much like it. The printer was a little terrier of a man and, in his capacity as editor of Tiedown's now-defunct newspaper, had sometimes waxed pretty pompous. But, to Jones' way of thinking, the feller was a windbag and more like to take his resentments out in talk than involve himself in this kind of dido. Gattison seemed too peppery to be possessed of either the patience or cunning.

Not that Jones didn't plan to have some words with him once the more urgent of his chores were out of the way. He planned to see Charco, too, but figured first of all he'd better get in touch with Grisswell. The most explosive element in this whole situation—as Butterfly saw it in his own mind—was that hired gunny, Raumeller, and if there was any way of parting him from Grisswell's company the sheriff reckoned he ought to do it before somebody got killed.

Jones wasn't particularly hungry when he plopped himself down on one of the Lone Star's stools, but he got into a conversation with the local Butterfield agent and became so engrossed in his speculations that before he got up he'd put away two eggs, a thick slab of steak, four pieces of toast, three cups of java and a pretty fair chunk of gooseberry pie. More miraculous still, he got shed of his headache.

Gattison, it seemed, had been making enquiries concerning stage connections which had necessitated checking with a number of other lines. While nothing appeared to be firm yet, and neither money nor ticket had crossed the counter, the points being aimed at—the agent told Butterfly—were Butte, Montana, and Deadwood in the Dakotas. Moreover the printer, Jones was told, had not even been near the Butterfield office. The go-between had been a nine-year-old, one of the Potter brood of broken-down whites camped out in Rag Holler ever since Trimbo had run them off a quarter section of Geetch's land.

This sort of thing looked pretty hush-hush to Jones and fetched several growls as he headed for the livery to pick up his horse. Thinking back he remembered the Potters had been moved three years ago . . . about the same time Spangler's crew had burnt the Olafsons out.

But if Gattison intended to shake the dust of this town why not just *do* it? Who was he trying to hide it from? Geetch?

"Trimbo . . ." Jones said, thoughtfully frowning. Strangely enough the man hadn't previously come into his consideration of possible suspects. Nor could Butterfly think why he'd so easily dismissed him after that business last night out back of Bernagrowt's.

It had been a mighty close thing he was grimly reminded, gingerly touching the nicked ear's abraded skin. Jones had let the man go in bitter disgust after Spangler got into it . . . because of the bluff Geetch's range boss had run with an empty gun?

There had been no proof Trimbo had taken the shot at him; no evidence on the other hand to prove that he hadn't, *and who was closer to Geetch than Trimbo?* Who would know better how to stir up Geetch's fury, how to play on his weaknesses, feed his angers? And it wasn't as though that un-fired iron the sheriff had unloaded gave the feller a clean bill of health. He could easily have had another cached about him. Jones remembered now he'd been intending to look—and a golrammed pity he hadn't!

The feller had been near enough—and at the right time, too, to have thrown those slugs that had killed the dude's mare. There were a number of things, Jones was suddenly discovering, which—with Trimbo as prime mover—appeared to drop into place.

All the time he was saddling up the sheriff poked and prodded Trimbo for size. He looked a pretty apt fit; the biggest thing really lacking, Jones concluded, was motive, and a little judicious digging might uncover that, too.

But Gattison, also, was beginning to make rather far-apart tracks. If these enquiries stemmed from the smashing of his press why was he being so secretive? And why hadn't he up and gone before this? The man had known straight off the press was irreparable. What dark facts could the man have nosed out?

If the press had been destroyed to put the paper out of business . . . Jones, shaking his head, went into the saddle. A hint drastic as that would have been sufficient to shut most mouths, and it appeared to have shut Gattison's. Jones, when he'd talked with him had certainly not got anything worth writing home about.

But if what he'd nosed out had been sufficiently damaging mightn't the printer have tried a bit of blackmail? This, in conjunction with the man's known character, seemed to Jones to be a reasonable assumption. Seemed to tie in, too, with those guarded enquiries into stage connections. So what was he waiting for?

The loot, of course!

It came down on Jones like a ton of brick. The man was waiting for the payoff.

The cocky little bastard!

With cold sweat breaking through the pores of his skin, Jones, suddenly snarling, kicked a grunt from his gelding. Half a minute later he jumped off at the middle of town and, knocking men off his elbows, bucked his way into the hotel-lobby, making straight for the desk in a spur-chinging stride.

"You seen Gattison this mornin'?"

Flancher looked startled, worriedly shook his head.

"What room's he in?"

"Second floor back—Number Ten . . ."

Jones took the stairs like a herd of buffalo, made the bend for the ell and banged on the panels of the door chalked 10. He got nothing but sore knuckles. Dang fool was probably gone to the cattle judging, but just to make sure he wasn't still abed sleeping, the sheriff tried the door and, finding it unlocked, shoved it open.

He saw the shape on the bed and swore.

Gattison wouldn't trouble no one anymore.

XVII

But, having locked the door and pocketed the key, Jones stood awhile, frowning, gone back in his thinking again to Trimbo and the dark shape of Spangler stiffly standing behind him. His breakfast was not riding too smooth and there was a brassy taste in his throat like bile. Be powerful easy to go off half-cocked.

And tramping down the stairs, with all those staring faces peering up at him, he couldn't help wondering at the strange compulsion he felt, even now, to heave away any hint of Geetch's guilt. Somebody sure as sin had took hold of that printer, angrily, viciously, to shut his mouth.

"Was he there?" Flancher asked.

"He was there," Jones said, and the whole damned lobby appeared to hang on his words. He beckoned Flancher aside. "Anyone asked fer 'im?"

The hotel man shook his head. "Something wrong?"

"You think there might be?"

"Well," Flancher grumbled, "you look kinda odd."

"Don't let it worry you, and stay away from that second floor. Don't let nobody up there. An' keep your lip buttoned. I'm sendin' Terrazas over soon as I can find him."

He went out on the porch, eyes quartering the street. He didn't know what he expected to find, but whatever it was he couldn't set his teeth in it. Things looked about the same . . . traffic a little heavier, maybe.

He moved down the steps and got on his horse, and presently turning him into the flow, sandwiched him through and cut left toward the jail. Quite a few of the jabberers he saw on the walks appeared to be drifting in the direction of the stockyards, though the races weren't scheduled to start before one.

A glance at his shadow showed it wasn't yet ten. Dismounting beside the jail he went into his office, his narrowed stare finding his deputy doodling at the desk. "Sort of figured you'd be out policing the street."

Terrazas, looking up, blew the sweat off his nose. "Didn't seem much use in both of us roasting. Saw you go past as I was—"

"Gattison," Jones said, "ain't no longer with us."

"You mean he packed up and—"

"Somebody scrambled his brains with the barrel of a six-shooter."

Astonishment twisted half the lines of Terrazas' face and then a blankness clamped down and his unreadable eyes considered Jones steadily while the clock on the wall continued solemnly to mark the passage of time. He said abruptly, "Gattison!" like it didn't make sense.

Though he was not quite able to put his fist on the reason, it got into Jones' mind there was something dimly off-key about this performance. "The guy tried to put somebody over a barrel. But he fiddled too long an' the heat caught up with him."

Terrazas' glance widened. "You suggesting he was trying to collect *hush* money?"

"Looks that way." Jones told the coroner what he'd found out from Butterfield's man. "He was fixin' t' skip soon's he feathered his nest. You better git over there."

He tossed Terrazas the key.

The man opened his mouth, apparently thought better of it, shrugged and departed.

Now what was he fixing to say? Jones wondered, pondering the coroner's final, dubious look. Likely something about Geetch.

Darkly scowling Jones hauled the sketch of Spangler from his pocket and, smoothing it out, studied, deeply uneasy, the penciled likeness. He found it pretty persuasive. The kind of look you'd expect to find on the face of a man who would beat another man's head in.

Still frowning, the sheriff climbed into the saddle. He didn't know what to do, really; whether to hunt up Grisswell or go see Geetch.

He peered at his watch. The hands said ten-thirty. Jones had never found Spangler an easy man to talk to and, remembering the way they had parted here last night, he entertained no illusions concerning his probable reception.

For the benefit of fairs the county had scraped a half-mile oval just north of the stockyards, erecting one rail of peeled poles—presently whitewashed— around this bullring's outside perimeter. On the nearer side, between it and the stockyard pens and chutes, a saddling paddock in the form of a wheel made of warped mesquite lengths had been thrown up beside ten tiers of jerry-built bleachers. Beyond the track's far side, amid considerable activity, were the flimsy, weatherbeaten structures locally known as Shed Row. It was for these, still scowling, that Jones pointed his horse.

Among mounds of baled hay, battered tubs of water, arridly pungent heaps of mixed manure and bedding, those involved went on with the chores attendant to getting a race under way. Flies were everywhere, buzzing and circling over refuse and feed, and the area was additionally cluttered by the curious, bookmakers and bettors and those who— the largest number—had gratuitously come to offer their counsel.

Off to one side Charlie Mullins was walking a powerful-looking black stallion with a white star and snip. Several other horse walkers slouched along in procession. Between these and her, Jones observed the Grisswell stable hand, Jeeter, eyes fiercely alert above the dark tubes of his twin-barreled Greener.

From the vantage of his saddle, Jones peered around, hoping to catch sight of Cathie's father, and presently did so. But the Gourd & Vine owner, when Jones' glance ran him down, was over by the sheds, deep in talk with Sig Raumeller. The sheriff watched them awhile, thinking Grisswell would presently be done and one or the other of them move to someplace which might allow a more casual approach. After fidgeting for several minutes under the stare of the gun fighter Jones wheeled his mount and went looking for Geetch.

He found the Quarter Circle S owner holding forth in a group of well-wishers who had money on his horse. The talk derisively revolved about Grisswell and the consensus of opinion seemed to have the dude's thoroughbred whipped to a standstill before he so much as set foot on the track.

Jones was reluctant to intrude on this pleasure but he had either to speak with someone pretty quick or wash his hands of the whole upsetting business, at least so far as trying to avert hostilities went.

Lips drawn into a distasteful grimace he kneed his horse over, hearing the talk fall away as people discovered his presence.

Spangler did not help him. With his pale squinted stare bleakly fixed on the sheriff the rancher stood waiting, belligerently silent, putting the whole burden of any exchange on Price Jones.

But Jones, now that he had the cattle king's attention, could not seem to find any reasonable approach. He had vaguely thought he might point out in a general sort of way the dangers the race could produce. Face to face with Geetch the whole idea looked a bit preposterous. Nor could he ask the rancher to withdraw from the race.

He cleared his throat self-consciously. "You fellers hear about Gattison gettin' knocked off?"

There was no sign of shock. Though Jones had put it to the group he'd kept his glance pinned to Geetch and got no change at all. A couple of the others looked mildly surprised but no one offered any vocal contributions.

"That's straight," Jones affirmed, cheeks beginning to burn. "I ain't pullin' your legs. He was found in his room at the Drover's Rest, dead in his bed with his head bashed in."

Spangler made no bones of his contemptuous indifference. "Small loss," he declared. "Man's been askin' for that ever since he come here." Then his stare beating harder against Jones' face, he said with an unmistakable sneer, "Did you reckon *I* had anything to do with it?"

That bleached-agate stare was no easy thing to meet and Jones visibly squirmed. But he did not back off. Fully seeing the trench he might be digging for himself, he told the cattle king, "Your past performances sure ain't been above reproach."

Spangler's neck and chest swelled while the rest stared askance and the rancher's bloating features took on the color of fury. Then a scornful bark of a laugh leaped out of him. "F' Christ's sake, Jones! When you goin' t' grow up?"

That was pretty hard to take, hard in any circumstance but doubly so with these yaps looking on, storing it up to pass around later. But Jones hung on, not letting Geetch throw him. "We're talkin' about you an' that dead guy, mister. You can talk t' me or you can talk to a warrant."

XVIII

To himself Jones sounded astonishingly firm, a hard-held restraint wearing noticeably thin in the harshening tones of that delivered ultimatum.

Sheerest kind of bluff. Inside, aghast, he was a quagmire of squirming, quivering contradictions, unsure even if he had any basis for threatening arrest.

And this blustery old man, no matter anything else, was still the county's Number One citizen, paying the most taxes, entitled by such to the veneration, allegiance and unfaltering support of each and every county official. They were all part and parcel of the Spangler power and influence, prerogatives of the mighty.

Preposterous twaddle? Well, perhaps. Certainly no such feudal notions could be found in the ordinances and lawbooks, but their shadows hedged in every lawman's horizon, circumscribing his authority, stronger than wire. And it looked like Geetch was desperate.

But Jones had *his* back against a wall, too. For if Spangler had any hand in what had happened to that printer he was almost certainly concerned with the rest—the Purple Cow stickup, the wrecking of Gattison's press, Ferguson's death and, by the same token, that pair of slugs which had been thrown at Grisswell. It was all of a piece in Price Jones' head and he was faced with the job of getting at the truth of it. *And if Geetch wasn't guilty he had the right to be cleared.*

The old man's look, still livid, seemed somehow more cagey, and now he said in a more disciplined way. "I'm a reasonable man. Ask your questions; I've got nothing to hide."

"Where was you last night?"

"Part of the time I was out to the ranch. Bulk of the night right here on Shed Row, rolled in my soogans hard ag'in that door." The lifted sweep of rope-scarred hand indicated the closed lower half of one of the stalls, over which a gray tail jerked occasionally at flies.

"You never went to the hotel?"

Spangler said, snorting, "With the kind of stakes I got sunk in this race you think I'd leave Eight Below here alone!"

"You could have left Trimbo with him."

"Trimbo was off uptown—you know that."

"I seem to recall seein' *you* uptown, too. At around ten o'clock in front of the jail. When the

three of us was havin' that powwow, who was
watchin' your horse?"

"I'd just rode the horse in—"

"You weren't mounted when I talked with you."

"The horse right then was with two of my boys.
They was right in plain sight if you'd troubled to
look."

Sweat lay damply across the ridges of Geetch's
cheeks and the cut of his glance was fast hardening
into intolerance. "Why pick on me? *I'm* not the one
that's been luggin' in gunslingers—matter of fact I
been lettin' men go."

"Yeah. I heard about that. About Mullins an' all
them I.O.U.'s. Looks like t' me you got your tail in
a crack," Jones remarked, looking the cattleman
spang in the eye. "While we're dealin' in facts suppose you tell *me* where you scraped up the money
you've bet on this race?"

Rage sprang in Spangler's apoplectic stare and
for one stunned moment he stood absolutely
speechless, the hamlike fists whitely clenched at his
sides. Then he cried in a voice that cracked with
wrath, "I don't hev to take that! I don't hev t' take
that crap off nobody!" And, roughly shouldering
past the shocked faces, the fellow stalked off like a
sore-footed bull.

Jones, peering after him, scrubbed a hand across
his jaw and then drew a ragged breath, nervously
echoed by others. But, unlike these, Jones was not
content sheepishly to stare at his boot toes. "Who's
he figure t' put on that horse?"

He got mostly shrugs and uneasy glances. But

one ranny, bolder or more gabby than the rest, undertook to say: "That Mex'kin, Tavares."

Something jumped inside Jones. "Tavares?"

"Charco, I believe his name is."

"Anyone know where a man could git hold of him?"

Someone else interrupted the tobacco chewer to say, "Last I seen they was headed fer town."

"Thanks," Jones said, and wheeled away.

Probably bound for some bar to pick up an early lunch. The very fact that Trimbo was with the man suggested Spangler was taking no chances on his jock getting plastered or being propositioned.

Since Trimbo's habits were common knowledge, Jones reckoned to find the pair holding down a table at the Aces Up. He considered it also a pretty safe bet the vaquero would be reluctant to do any talking in front of his range boss. Nor could Butterfly see any way to get around this.

It wasn't likely the man could add anything important to what Terrazas had already told him; and when he reached this point in his cogitations Jones was minded to forget the whole thing.

But the basis of any efficient police system was the routine check, so he guessed he'd better get on with it. While a habla with the coroner's cousin probably wouldn't turn up a single new fact, it might at least get a few of the loose ends straightened out.

He slipped off his horse in front of the saloon, but just as he was about to push through the bat-wings he spied Cathie Grisswell coming down the street behind matched bays in the Gourd & Vine surrey. She saw him too and, smiling brightly, waved.

It was a friendly thing, and doubly so to a man deeply mired in Jones' thankless job. He stepped back into the street and when she pulled up, set an anchoring boot on the nearest hub. "An' how's the wildlife treatin' you, Miz' Cathie?" he asked, unconsciously comparing her with the home-town product.

"Why, that's just what I was about to ask *you!*" she laughed. A woman of the world, she had no trouble assessing the wistful admiration so transparent in his glance. Her own eyes teased, while the world stood still and Jones dredged up the lugubrious grimace of a winded swimmer going down for the final count.

"I don't suppose," she said, "you've seen Mr. Raumeller?"

Jones' expression parched, and beneath the surface he twitched like a fish at first feel of steel. "That golrammed gunny—"

"Oh, Sig's not so bad," she broke in to say defensively—"not when you *understand* him, I mean . . ." and sort of sighed into silence, peering a little uncertain at the look on Jones' face. But Cathie, in the East, had found an answer for everything. Her red lips sprang apart in a dazzling smile, and she reached down to give him an affectionate pat. "Silly! I have a message from Daddy," she explained. "Wouldn't you like to ride along?"

"Some other time," Jones said; then, rather bleakly, "Expect you'll find 'em over on Shed Row."

He touched his hat and stepped back, feeling about as sociable as a centipede with chilblains. How could a woman *be* so taken in as she was?

He went into O'Halleran's and found the Irishman back of the bar. Bellying up, Jones called for a double and took it neat with a toss of the head. Squinting into the glass his stare went past the float of hats, on over the games to find Trimbo hunched at one of the tables with a bottle, two glasses, but no sign of a companion. The feller, of course, might have stepped out back.

While Jones was trying to think what to do, some jasper three shapes to the left of him called: "H'are ya, Tavares! What's that nag gonna do?"

"Quien sabe, señor . . . ?"

Jones spotted him then, over by the free lunch, a flash of teeth under a chin-strapped hat with a snakeskin band. He had a slight, wiry figure garbed in cowpuncher clothes; and then Jones had hold of him, watching the grin drop off Tavares' face.

Shoving him back a couple of steps the sheriff saw Trimbo coming up with a scowl. Butterfly, waving him off, growled, "Keep out of this, buster!" but Spangler's hardcase kept coming, big hands fisted, eyes hateful.

He came in swinging. Jones used his gun. The barrel caught Trimbo just back of an ear. Spangler's man folded. Jones shoved Tavares toward the green slatted doors.

Outside he said: "All right, let's have it. What's my deputy got against Geetch?"

The man licked dry lips. "He took the ranch of my cousin's father—eet was the firs' place he grab."

"Damn!" Jones muttered, Tavares' disclosure still slapping him in the teeth as he reined away. This certainly opened a whole Pandora's box of disturbing possibilities.

The strongest motive still sat in Geetch's corner, but who could say how long hard thoughts had been hidden and festering in the coroner's mind? It sure must have happened a good piece back, Jones himself having no recollection of it, but a dispossessed heir would not have forgotten. The knife must have turned every time he saw Spangler.

While Jones was still woolling it around through his thoughts, Geetch Spangler, filled with sound and fury and forking the horse he had set out to race, came ramming head-on through the scraggles of traffic. The man's bulging orbs smacked into Butterfly like bullets and, with his horse hauled hard back on its haunches—"Jones!" Spangler yelled in the quavery voice of a gut-shot gopher on his last whistling breath.

The sheriff winced.

The cattleman sat wheezing on his sweat-drenched mount, every eye fastened on him, nobody moving out of their tracks. A woman's strident laughter coming out of the Aces Up tinnily tinkled across the street's sudden hush. Spangler's twisted mouth worked and Jones said reluctantly, "What's chewing you, Geetch?"

"That goddam dude! You know what he's done? Throwed a dam across the Verdigris an' cut off my water!"

XIX

A jag of wild thoughts stampeded across the windy funnel of Jones' mind. His eyes kind of glazed and then he shook himself like a dog shedding water. "You know this fer sure?"

"Alls I know is one of my men just rode in with—"

"He say the river's plumb dry?"

"Said there's less'n two inches of water comin' through! All summer we been gettin' the better part of—"

"But there *is* water?" Jones cut in.

"About a inch an' a half," Spangler said through his teeth.

"Then I don't see much the law can do about it. Your man see the dam?"

"You're golrammed right! Four miles up river. They had three guys watchin' it with rifles!"

"Well," Jones said, "I'll speak to him—"

"Speak, hell!" Geetch snarled like a rabid wolf. "I'll—"

He broke off, darkly staring, as the sheriff fetched a rummaging hand from his pocket, holding out an open fist to show a pair of discolored-brass cartridge cases. "You recognize these?"

The rancher, motionless, stared. "Shells from a Sharps, ain't they?"

"You know anyone that's got a Sharps they'll fit?"

Geetch, looking suddenly old, tiredly sighed. His eyes peered around and then came back to Jones' face. "Expect you know the answer to that. The only Sharps in this country them shells fit is mine." He turned silent a moment. "You prob'ly won't believe it but I ain't fired that gun in more'n two years."

Jones said, "You mind if I have a look at it?"

"I don't hev the gun no more."

"You know what these shells was fired at?"

Spangler said, "I kin guess."

"Have a try."

"They either killed that printer or Grisswell's mare. But *I* never fired 'em," Spangler doggedly declared.

Jones, after a moment, dropped the shells in his pocket. He didn't say whether he believed the man or not. He swung into the saddle and reined his horse toward the jail.

But, part way there, he found himself suddenly needing a word with Charlie Mullins, and cut over past the stock pens, scowlingly turning something over in his head.

In the stable area he found the crowd considerably large. Jubal Jo had his black head over the stall's Dutch door, ears cocked as though profoundly taking in the things Hollister Grisswell was telling his trainer. All Jones caught was his didactic tone before the medicine king, discovering him, took the thick cigar from his expressive mouth to smile.

"And how is Price Jones this morning?" he said easily. "I trust the cares of the shrievalty will not interfere with the display of velocity we're about to witness. I was just remarking to Miss Mullins what a pity it is so many of these people in their clannish distrust of a man from outside—"

"You honestly think," Jones growled, "you're goin' to *win* that race?"

"I consider it self-evident. My dear fellow," Grisswell sighed in his most patronizing fashion, "the chances of Jubal losing are practically nonexistent. He has a reach of twenty-six feet, covering that much ground at a single jump." The girl, when he glanced at her for confirmation, nodded. "Spangler, and these yokels that are backing him, are pinning their faith on the notion that a short horse, closer to the ground, will get off on top and achieve full speed in from two to three jumps."

"You don't believe it?"

"I think, in most instances, I would have to agree with the assumption. But," Grisswell smiled, "Jubal—for a hotblood—has a very fast break.

Spangler's horse won't gain enough at the outset to overcome the black's greater reach. If you've any spare money jingling around in your pockets I'd advise you to get on him."

Jones, after eyeing him carefully, said, "Did you know we'd found that horse Geetch lost?"

"Really?" Grisswell said, barely showing polite interest. "It rather seems to me the whole business of that horse has had no other purpose than deliberately to embarrass me—"

"That why you cut off his water?"

Above pursed lips Grisswell's look became flinty.

"Is there nothing that fellow won't do to gain his ends? Look—" he said irritably, "I haven't cut off his water. Why don't you ride out there and see for yourself? I have simply diverted my own legal share —which I have every right to do."

"It's not like t' make you many friends around here."

"Friends!" Grisswell scoffed. "How naive can you get?" One hand slid into his coat and came out to hold up a fancified red-leather wallet. With a short, snorting bark of a laugh he said, "Here are the only friends *I*'ve encountered."

"That's a pretty hard view."

"It's a pretty hard world." The Gourd & Vine owner put his pocketbook away. "I'm a practical man. I'm willing to recognize facts. The facts of this business are plain. And I intend to protect myself."

Jones said gruffly, "Are you accusin'—"

"I wouldn't waste my breath."

Jones shifted uneasily in the crotch of his saddle. "You've got no proof—"

Grisswell said across the curl of his lip, "You can tell that fellow, anything he tries will be paid back in the same coin with compound interest. He's not dealing this time with poor whites and Mexicans!"

XX

Trimbo came up and Grisswell, beckoning, took him off out of earshot while Jones, plainly fuddled, was trying to pull himself together.

"Maybe, if you'd talk to Geetch—" Charlie Mullins began, but Jones shook his head.

"Might's well try t' scratch my neck with my elbow," he muttered disgustedly, and sat a moment scowling, looking at her but obviously not seeing her. "Why'd you quit him?"

"I was tired, I guess . . ." Her voice trailed away, and then she said, more vigorously, "You asking for the truth or—"

Jones, breaking loose of a look he'd encountered before, hurriedly gathered up his reins, mumbled something unintelligible, kicked his horse into a lope and, slightly red of cheek, departed.

Not until he'd gotten clean away from the stable

area did he let his mount ease or draw a truly free breath.

Grisswell had disturbed him—no getting around that. But the look he'd caught in Rockabye's stare was the kind no bachelor was like to tempt more of —no guy, anyway, with all of his buttons. Jones could pretty near hear the skreak of double harness!

It was plain that dude had offered more dough than Spangler had been of any mind to pay her. Feller seemed to think his money could get him just about anything; and it crossed Jones' mind to wonder right then how much of the dude's money was responsible for this star.

It was a sobering thought, not an easy one to live with.

And thinking over a number of other remarks the man had let drop in the course of their acquaintance, Butterfly found himself heading down into Rag Holler, a firetrap of whoppy-jawed tents and ramshackle shanties. It proved no great bother to locate the Potter clan, but getting Potter to unburden himself appeared about as unlikely as anything Jones had yet come up against. The man wasn't looking for trouble and said so.

"I'm not here t' make trouble," declared Jones testily. "Alls I want is a talk with them kids."

"They don't know nothin'."

"Where's that boy you call Dub?"

"What's he done now?" the boy's father whined, bristling.

Jones drew a pair of silver dollars from his

pocket, chunking them suggestively from one hand to the other. "That him over there? The one without no shirt?"

Potter sullenly nodded.

"Dub," Jones said, "you kin do the law a favor if you'd say straight out where you toted them notes you got from Mr. Gattison."

The boy, eyes puckered against the sky's livid glare, cocked his head to one side and asked, curling his lip, "What's the law ever done fer the likes of us?"

It appeared to Jones, trying to find a fair answer, that all the hard views were not necessarily held by the moguls of this community. Scrubbing his jaw he shot a grim look at Potter, reconsidered the boy and presently said soberly, "The law's like a old man needin' new spectacles. Means well, I reckon, but t' be of much use he's got t' have the help of fellers whose eyes is still sharp an' clear. There ain't nothin' wrong with *your* eyes, I'll warrant."

The boy, sniffing scornfully, refused to be drawn.

Jones, sighing, took a page from Grisswell's book and held up the silver dollars. "Tell you what I'll do, Dub. I'll swap you these two cartwheels t' have an' spend as you see fit if you'll tell me where you took them notes."

"Took 'em to the Post Office."

Jones, frowning, said, "They was *letters?*"

"Sure had stamps on 'em."

"When you got to the Post Office what'd you do?"

"Pushed 'em through the slot." Dub, advancing, nervously put out a hand and Jones slipped him the coins.

But he wasn't licked yet. There was still Terrazas, and all the way back to town he considered the man they had given him for deputy, and the words of his cousin, the vaquero whose ingenuity or patience had turned up the missing pony. He even dug out the likeness the coroner had drawn of Geetch and stared a grim while at its uncomplimentary aspects.

"Eet was the firs' place he grab," the cowboy, Charco, had said.

With that kind of thing always clawing a man, Jones did not find it too tough to understand why Terrazas could appear so convinced Geetch himself was behind all the things which appeared to be frothing up around them. The man would naturally suspect Geetch; but was that the whole shape of it? Or was Terrazas more deeply committed? Embittered, revengeful, had the man in his brooding hatred of Spangler gone so far as to attempt to steer what was happening?

Certain aspects seemed to suggest he had. There was the night—*last night, actually*—when Jones in his anger had had that run-in with Trimbo. When, disgusted, he had left the Spangler ramrod and Geetch himself at the jailhouse steps to come into the office and find Terrazas in the dark with a loaded Greener.

The explanation the deputy had offered, now that Jones was able to take a good look at it, seemed pretty feeble—even kind of unlikely. And there were other things, too, that seemed to click into place as the sheriff traced back through the past several hours a whole series of instances that now appeared a little queer.

Had those letters Dub posted been delivered to Terrazas?

But what was the point in running off with that pony horse? To spur up bad feeling between the two moguls? To drive Geetch into some open attack?

And the gunfighter, Raumeller . . . Had Terrazas been the go-between in securing his services for Grisswell?

The sheriff was plagued by no dearth of questions, but the continuing tramp of his unruly thoughts refused to turn up any very convincing answers. On evidence available Spangler still looked to be the number one choice. The cowman's bullypuss ways had ridden roughshod over too many persons other people remembered, and financially at least, the man appeared in bad shape, reduced even to letting a full half of his crew go.

In such circumstances, Jones asked himself, where had the feller laid hands on the money he'd put up with the barkeeps, trying to get well on the outcome of this race? From that Purple Cow holdup? From the pockets of bushwhacked Harley Ferguson?

The sheriff, growling in his throat, morosely pawed at his cheeks as he took in the clabbering jostle of people all bound with their gab in the direction of the track.

He was aware that time was about to run out.

Dreading to see this race come off, he could think of no handle he could pull to stop it. It looked to him to be synonymous with disaster and, unless he could block it, was almost sure to end in gunplay. This was purely hunch, stirred by his conviction the stakes put up had got entirely too high. Geetch's horse, in this go, was a nine-to-one favorite, but if the nag failed to win just about anything could happen—and all of it unpleasant.

If Spangler wasn't behind all the things Jones could sense rushing headlong to a boil, then the stage was surely set by one whose obvious intention was to see the cattleman blamed for it. Question was *who*? Give him the answer to that and the chance to get at the guy, he just might be able to stop this fracas short of a killing . . . but he didn't believe it.

There seemed so many loose ends, so many explosive possibilities. Grisswell with his money and his bitterness toward the town . . . How much of this could be tracked back to him? And Geetch, and that Sharps the cattleman claimed he didn't have anymore. Since *when* hadn't he had it?

A man didn't know whether to believe the old wolf or put him down for a plain-out liar. But Jones, as sheriff, could not afford to stall any longer. He had to take chips. He had to step out on one side or the other, to pick his man and abide by the consequences. And at last, still reluctant, he made up his mind.

XXI

Most sprints in the days before starting gates—
particularly matched affairs cooked up between
owners—took a considerable while to get on the
road, and the one in hand at the Tiedown bullring,
as the riders interminably jockeyed for position,
did little to mollify the buildup of tensions.

After a hectic hour spent abortively in scoring,
with the sun beating down and the furies of frustration loosening restraint, all the goriest fears at the
back of Jones' thoughts looked scarcely a hand's
span from grim realization.

The shouts and catcalls of the crowd grew ugly.
No one with money up was minded to leave, and it
was increasingly clear they would not tolerate
much longer delay. Grisswell's black, fairly trembling with impatience, showed a froth white as
soap between satiny cheeks while he fought the bit,

sidling, under the girl's tight rein.

The gray Eight Below, Spangler's entry, appeared in somewhat better case but the wiry Charco, perched on his sear singer, seemed like a cornered rat, as his dripping face kept twisting desperate glances across the cant of a protectively hunched shoulder.

What was he scared of?

Afraid Geetch had taken too much out of the horse? Or was he signed up to lose and starting to panic about his chances of getting clear in the event he went through with it?

Jones, thus reminded of Grisswell's attitude, took his own assessment of the possibilities. This crowd—should they suspect they had been sold out—was in no mood either to forgive or forget; and the sheriff, just in case the guy did try to run, was sorely tempted to get back in the saddle, only barely deterred by his notions about Geetch.

Nerved up, distrustful of his own convictions, he remained uncertainly watching, not too far from Spangler who was scowlingly peering toward where the dude stood with his hired gun and buggy boss.

As the riders wheeled back to once again take positions Cathie Grisswell, enticingly garbed in Eastern bridle-path toggery, came up to take Jones' arm with a proprietary smile. "They will surely get away pretty soon, don't you think?"

Jones, without peeling his glance off Geetch, gruffly said he didn't know, and looking somewhat fussed, managed to free his pistol hand despite her attempt to keep hold of it. She said, looking up at him, "What's the matter with you?"

A thud of hoofs brought dust boiling up off the course and Jones, craning his neck, might have been completely alone for all the notice he took of her. Attention had jumped to the main event and he could see the two riders bearing down on the score. As they came up to the line Charlie Mullins cried: "Ready?" and Charco Tavares, on the gray, shouted, "*Go!*"

Spangler's short horse, under the quirt, crossed the score like something heaved from a catapult, rocketing into a barreling lead that appeared somewhat greater than a full length of daylight. The crowd roared approval and the Mexican, hand-riding, pushed his advantage another half length and he kept that edge for the next twenty jumps. And then Grisswell's black began cutting it down, just as the dude had told Jones he would.

The yells died away. They flashed past the eighth pole, Jubal Jo, driving, scarcely a length behind the gray. And Rockabye Mullins hadn't yet used her bat.

It was sickening the way that big black ate up ground. Every stride seemed to chip away more of the gray's lead. A dozen jumps past the pole brought the thoroughbred's nose almost even with Eight Below's flying tail. And then the black, still driving, began to inch toward his flank. Charco—apparently almost beside himself—was furiously belaboring the gray with his quirt, first one side and then on the other, but the black kept gaining.

"Throw that damn whip away!" Jones could hear Spangler yelling through the crowd's lifted groans but the Mexican, face livid, kept beating his mount as though it was the only prescription for victory he knew.

The black's froth-flecked muzzle now had reached the gray's shoulder and the hard-flogging pound of those racing hoofs had scarcely another fifty yards to go. Every man in that incensed crowd was on his feet, most of them running after the horses toward the finish.

Only Geetch hadn't budged, nor the group about Grisswell whose features had taken on a kind of smug blankness. The gunfighter's stare was fixed abrasively on Geetch. The Gourd & Vine buggy boss, Eldon Shores, dropped several words from the side of his face which the former purveyor of bottled nostrums seemed to find humorous enough for a laugh.

These were the happy ones. The smart city slickers who had tailored a coup and now could lay back and wax fat on their profits—perhaps even pleased at the plight of this town, wholly indifferent to the havoc they had wrought.

Jones' attention veered back to the track. Now the black nose showed against the gray's head, both of them pouring their all into this effort, closing the gap between themselves and the wire with ears pinned back and wide, gaping nostrils. The thunder of hoofs beat against Jones' thoughts. So close together were the two horses here it almost seemed as though their riders were crouched knee to knee, cursing or praying or whatever people did when the chips were down and the spoils for the victor only short gasps away. Charco, apparently, had lost his quirt and the gray's stride had lengthened, seeming less choppy as neck and neck they plunged toward that final moment of truth.

It was the girl's arm now that had gone to the whip, expertly reaching back to touch the black just once . . . and then again, more sharply, as she sought in the memory of other times to push that dark nose into the lead. You could see the horse strain—leastwise Jones thought he could, but as they swept round the turn he could still see the edge of one gray nostril beyond the open-jawed muzzle of the black. And that was the way they crossed the finish, with the flag swooping down and the banker through his megaphone crying out the race in favor of Jubal Jo.

Geetch, with his purpling face, looked crazy—as mule-headedly crazy as a lot of these people had always figured him to be. Yelling, cursing, waving his arms like some bloody mad ape, he went stumbling blindly in the direction of Gretchen as though minded in his outrage to tear the banker limb from limb.

It came over Jones that even a walloper insensible as Geetch might sometimes feel much deeper than you'd think and maybe occasionally— like right here—be able to recognize right from wrong. And one thing more Jones saw, that most of his own notions had fallen short of the truth.

Sure he'd picked his man and in the main been

right. Certainly greed and avarice—even, perhaps, some element of revenge, had shown their pinched and parfleche faces. But only indirectly had the core of this squabble leaned toward either range or dollars.

It was sprung from the head, a nasty matter of ego, evolved from twists almost impossible to track down. Driven of course by ambition, but promulgated in a mind that refused to consider accepted truths. This fellow in *his* view was Mr. Big; there was no middle ground that he was willing to stand on. He was a man who had to be first every time, a man wholly ready to kill to make sure of it.

Catching up the reins of the first mount he came to, Price Jones went into the saddle, knowing this bastard had got to be stopped.

The stage was certainly set for murder. In the angry group around the flag-holding banker, Harold Terrazas stood with his Greener like Moses about to destroy the Golden Calf. The twin tubes of that sawed-off iron firm at his hip—having driven back the clamorous mob several paces— were now grimly leveled at the Spangler waistline, and it was plain from his expression the coroner-deputy needed mighty little more encouragement to shoot.

Jones, forcing his borrowed horse into this gathering, bitterly tried to move the crowd back some more, a task which met with very little success as resentful losers by the banker's decision furiously cursed his unwanted interference. And over and

149

above all the rest of this uproar the cowman's bull voice like a trumpet from Jericho was bludgeoning the din with the contumelious details of the banker's alleged ancestry.

The man's pasty face showed the pinched grip of fright as he was jostled and shoved by the hands reaching for him; and Jones, minded to bargain off a little skunk for a bigger one, dropped from the saddle to ram a gun in Geetch's ribs, thus at one stroke considerably diminishing the racket. While the cowman, confused, was twisting his head around, Jones said into the relative quiet: "Git back, you fellers, afore somebody gits hurt!" and, ere the bewildered ranchman could take in what he was up to, he had stepped back himself with a hog-leg leveled in each rope-scarred fist.

"Here—" Spangler yelled, "what'd you grab my gun fer?"

Jones, ignoring him, snapped at Terrazas, "Git a rope for our friend the chief commissioner," and saw T. Ed Gretchen begin to shake.

With his penurious eyes almost starting from his head the banker cried: "God, boys—not that!"

An approving chorus of growls from the crowd noisily engulfed whatever desperate appeal the banker in his terror might have made. Some of those faces looked pretty grim indeed until Jones, rather sternly, held up a gun-filled hand.

"How many of you figure that decision was fair an' right?"

Not a sound came out of that mob of scowling faces.

The vociferous shouts of those wedged round him must have washed out any last hopes the banker had. He almost collapsed. In a quavery croak scarcely louder than a gopher's he perspiringly admitted he might have been mistaken. "It was awful close. . . . I guess it could have been a . . ." he said hopefully, "a *tie?*"

Jones could almost pity him, pleading for belief. The look of the man embarrassed him. It was hard to reconcile this Ed Gretchen with the pompous fool of so many self-righteous pronouncements, the Simon Legree of so many hard bargains, the county commissioner so prone to foreclose on any poor slob who couldn't pay up.

But Jones hardened his heart, helped with this by the man's final perfidy which would have made paupers of at least half the town. "Why don't you tell them the truth," he said, "an' confess you knew dang well you was lyin'?"

"I couldn't help it!" he cried. "I had *three thousand*—" and choked, looking aghast at what he'd said.

"Now," Jones growled, "we're gettin' down t' cases. So you had three thousan' bucks on that race. A pillar of the Church. T. Ed Gretchen, the man who never gambles—"

"But I had no choice! I— You've got to believe me! I was *forced*—"

"I'll buy that if you'll make a clean breast of—"

"What's this?" Grisswell growled, coming up with Shores and a lynx-eyed stare from his fight-for-pay killer.

Jones looked them over. "Bein's you asked I don't mind sayin' your buddy, El Gretchen here, has just admitted he miscalled that race. Claimed first off it was your horse won; now it seems he was beat by—"

"What are you trying to pull?" the dude cried.

"*I* ain't tryin' t' pull anythin', mister, an' I don't wanta have t' kill someone over it, but until Gretchen's change of heart gits looked into, the law's goin' t' have to impound all bets. Unless," Jones observed, "you'd be willin' to abide by what your jock says."

"Charlie Mullins?" The dude laughed. Then he took another less-assured look at the man with the pistols. "Why wouldn't I be willing?"

"I don't think she'll lie."

Grisswell's jowls colored up like a gobbler's, and you could see the bluster shaping up in his face. Then, scowling again at Jones' guns, he said testily, "There's no occasion for lies—"

"My sentiments exackly."

The dude, suddenly uneasy, slanched a look at his firepower. "What are you talking about?"

"You," Jones said, "an' a couple of murders. One Harley Ferguson, fer instance, an' a black-mailin' printer. Put the cuffs on him, Terrazas," he barked at his deputy and, swiveling his artillery, brought Sig Raumeller into sharp focus.

Still holding his breath he was beginning to think he might yet bring this off, when everything seemed to come unstuck at once.

Geetch, with a beller that must have reached

clean to Tombstone, lunged for the dude like a
Green Bay Packer. At precisely this moment
Grisswell himself—sold short in Jones' shift to im-
mobilize the greater threat—slammed into the
sheriff with a fluttery squawk that swept one pistol
completely out of his grasp and flung him staggering into his mount.

The horse's head went down, his hind legs flew
up. The crowd broke apart in forty directions, each
guy and his neighbor frantically ducking for cover
as Raumeller's guns, jumping into his fists, commenced bucking and banging like an emplacement
of howitzers.

Something plucked at Jones' sleeve, something
jerked at his boot. Rolling desperately to get clear
of those flying hoofs he got off two shots and was
trying to get up with no idea of their effect when
the deafening double blast of the coroner's shotgun
whooshed past his face to knock Raumeller sprawling and drive all lesser sounds into oblivion.

Later, with Grisswell safely locked in a cell,
Jones—pouring drinks from the office bottle—sat
around with Terrazas and a mellowing Spangler,
hashing over the fracas. "Well, I was right after
all," the cowman said with authority, "that dang
dude *did* make off with my pony horse!"

"Someone from Gourd an' Vine did," Jones
nodded. "The idea, of course, was t' git all the
mileage they could from your rep while fixin' it t'
seem you was out t' bust Grisswell, lookin' fer any
excuse you could find. An' them I.O.U.'s you been

passin' around sure made it look like you was scrapin' rock bottom."

"I was kinda pinched," the cowman admitted, "tryin' to hold back enough cash to bet on that race."

"What I can't make out," Terrazas said, "is how you got onto that dude in the first place. What made you think it was him that was pushing this?"

"I didn't, straight off. It was buyin' up Spangler's notes on top of the way he had tailored that race, gettin' handbills printed in advance like he done, that finally set me t' diggin' around. Then that hullaballoo about him gittin' shot at with everyone knowin' Geetch had that kinda gun."

"But *why?*" the coroner growled. "The guy had plenty dinero—"

"That's what had me fightin' my hat. It was plain he hadn't no use fer Geetch, then I found out what he thought of this town—hated everything about it an' everyone in it. That didn't seem t' make much sense till it come over me the town had no time fer him either. But everyplace I looked it seemed like Geetch was the focal point, the prime target of all that was happenin'. That's when I realized the guy had a screw loose. He *had* t' be first; he couldn't abide t' stand in someone else's shadder."

Geetch said, "What's his girl goin' to do—anyone hear?"

"Understand she's packin'. Guess she's goin' back East. She's put the ranch up fer sale."

Geetch, swishing the whisky around in his

tumbler, had been studying Terrazas in a covert sort of way. Now he said across Jones to him, "If I was t' buy it, would you run the place fer me?"

The sheriff, reckoning this was about as near as the old wolf could come to fiddling around with an olive branch, got up with his bottle and stepped out on the porch, and just in time, as it happened, to observe Charlie Mullins slouching past on her old red roan.

Answering his wave she rode over to the steps. "When you gonna quit poisonin' yourself?"

Jones, scowling, said, "Just as a matter of idle curiosity, which nag you reckon really won that go?"

"Jubal did, by a lip an' two whiskers."

"I hope t' hell," Jones said, "you ain't passin that around."

Charlie Mullins laughed. "I figure to think about it some. You hear about that hoedown the folks is gettin' up for Saturday a week? If you was to come by an' really put your mind to it, I could prob'ly be persuaded."

ROGUE'S RENDEZVOUS

NELSON NYE

ROGUE'S RENDEZVOUS

NELSON NYE

ace books

A Division of Charter Communications Inc.
A GROSSET & DUNLAP COMPANY
51 Madison Avenue
New York, New York 10010

ROGUE'S RENDEZVOUS

I

Grimed and testy, with a rime of dried sweat showing white at the armpits, Jeff Kitchim pulled up to peer from disbelieving, beard-stubbled cheeks back across twenty yards of hoof-pocked road to find the girl still watching.

A provocative sight in her gypsy finery—scarlet, yellow and white against the mud wall of Arristo's Cantina. Slim, willow straight and tall for a gitana, though perhaps that high comb might account for some of this. Hair glimmery black as the sheen of a grackle's neck. Whitest teeth and boldest stare Kitchim had seen in a damned weary while; and he grinned at her, nodding, saw her thoughts close him out as, with lifted chin, she put back a hand to reach for the door.

Unexpectedly childlike, in the entrance she paused, eyes round as marbles, to appraise him again. Before she ducked out of sight, red lips pulled apart in a brighter flash of teeth, and there was nothing of a child in that gamin grin.

Kitchim, staring, swore.

Flirt with him, would she? He was minded, by grab! to go in there after her.

Jeff Kitchim had been a long time away from women.

Thinking tiredly back he scrubbed a hand across his face and, picking up the reins, kneed the floundering horse between flanking hovels. Everything seemed a long while, thinking back.

He felt about ten years older than Moses.

He'd never set out to become a hired gun. He guessed, halfway scowling, he had kind of fell into it. Impatient to get ahead, to have a spread of his own, he'd found orthodox ways too snail-like and slow. He'd courted quick money, and there'd been plenty of that available to fools.

No brains required. All a gun boss demanded to shell out fighting wages was a quick trigger finger and a scarcity of scruples.

Jeff had qualified early and now, at twenty-eight, was beginning to wonder if he'd backed the wrong horse. All across Texas the law was moving in. Owners who'd considered him survival insurance were lately finding Kitchim's presence embarrassing.

He hadn't encountered any dodgers carrying his particulars but that axe could fall anytime. Posted men were getting common as fleas and several who might recognize him were presently being whitewashed to pack Ranger tin.

Looking about, Jeff grimaced. Wasn't much of a place to come so far to get to. A manyanner town of flat-topped adobes—half of them unplastered. Only three miles north of the river's present banks. El Federico. Last time he'd been through this country—five years ago—El Federico had been Mexican-held but now, since the Rio had gouged a new channel, the subsequent "banco" on which the town stood had become, through treaty, a part of the sprawling Lone Star State. It was why he'd returned. What had happened once could happen again if the right kind of storm hit the river some night and this time maybe, if the cards broke right, he could make the big stake which had thus far eluded him.

Was that asking too much? Jeff Kitchim didn't think so on his hard-used horse. He had no other prospect if he couldn't make it here. Chancy? Of course—but he'd taken bigger chances for a whole lot less.

Striking south, toward the river, he rode with eyes half shut against the glare. The day's heat came out of the sandy earth in scriggly waves that danced like film against the gray-blue of far-off hills. There was nothing around him but pear and catclaw and tatters of amber forage grass, and, here and there, sticking up the gray wands of wolf's candle or the gnarled dwarf shape of an occasional mesquite.

A lonely land. Hot and dry and, for the most part, forgotten, given over to cattle and coyotes and the legless snakes that were native to it—which was all right with Kitchim.

His tough cheeks reflected a secret humor as he peered around seeking landmarks to figure from, and angling his mount a little more to the west.

In talk with others who had been through here he'd been told the new channel made a rather sharp loop around an outcrop of granite in this general direction, possibly two miles from town, and he wanted to have a look at this before getting down to cases with Fell.

He had already marked the river's old course with its straggly line of dying cottonwoods and willows—had even got down and tramped round through the stones below where the rampage had quit its last bed to gouge the new channel. It did not add a great deal to what he'd previously guessed. The river had left its banks at a bend.

One thing a man had to say for Kitchim—he was thorough, leaving nothing to chance which patience or hard work could bend to his favor. He had gained that much in these past nine years.

But there were facets of his character not easily bridled. The wild streak in him which had made him what he was still rebelled upon occasion, unsettling better judgments. That recklessness—at once his strength and bitterest weakness—was the albatross fate had hung about his neck, and it was this which had kept him chained to his rut.

Breasting a thicket of squatting cedars he came up in his stirrups to rake a long stare across the dun, heat-hazed miles. It had to be out there somewhere between his horse and those domes and spires, the ragged edges of slides, the gaunt outlines of chimneys and eroded bluffs lying red, chalky yellow and five shades of ocher against the gray shapes of those southernmost hills. He wasn't thinking now of the river but of the prize tucked away among these sunbaked wastes.

Riding on with his shadow through the late afternoon, cursing the heat and those lost younger years, he was forced once again to the hateful conclusion that his kind had outlived their use in this country and that, regrettably, guns were about all he knew. He had to make it this trip or bid goodbye to all hope for any better tomorrows. Had to make it now or cross the last thin line between what he had been and the sorry damn prospect of cashing in his chips at the end of somebody's rope.

II

He came down off high ground to tie his horse in the shinnery, afterwards peering through half-shut eyes to look rather grimly at the dream which had fetched him these many miles; the mud-brown river —sluggish now from months of drought but a roaring tiger in the time of rains, the tumbled rocks and parchment growth and beyond, the irrigated greenery of peon-worked fields and orchards . . . the red-tiled roofs and bell tower of Luis Capistrano's Hacienda Bavinuchi.

A kingdom balanced on the caprice of a river. Bavinuchi was cattle and wool and hides, storehouses, stables, shops and barns, a village, an empire—*a goddam way of life,* Kitchim thought, staring in open-faced envy. Hell for the peasants but a heaven on earth for those who stood at the top of the ladder. A pearl beyond price, but the pearl could be his if he played his cards right and had any luck at all.

He'd remembered the look of it all these months ... the stone saints and scrolls, the dusty plaza, the great house standing silent amid its garlands of flowers. The work office, commissary, farflung tangle of adobe corrals, the thick-walled quarters of Capistrano's mayordomo. The huts and shacks of the paisanos who toiled in ignorance even as their fathers before them had toiled among the hayfields and vineyards, the pens and pastures ... wherever ordered to increase the Capistrano wealth and well being. A feudal empire—his for the taking.

Snorting, Kitchim wheeled back to his horse. His for the taking, but only *if* and *providing* quite a number of things. Not all of which, unfortunately, depended on himself.

Climbing into the saddle he stood up to stare again, then kneed the big dun down a cattle trail which wound through the brush in the direction of the river. The bank proved too high at this point for his purpose and he was forced to ride west, well back from the crumbly rim, until the bluff toughened up enough to permit cautious passage. And thus he came presently to the bastion of granite about which the river had been flung, growling, north.

He could see at once that no amount of storms were going to break up any barrier as rugged as this—not, at any rate, within his lifetime. No wall of turgid water was going to leap this bend and he might just as well make up his mind to it. Acknowledging this, Kitchin turned his horse to look for other possibilities. And, backtracking, came within the hour to a curious convolution of the channel's tortuous course.

Kitchin, leaving the river, excitedly climbed to higher ground and dug the telescope out of his blankets. From this vantage, working the glass, he was able to bring Bavinuchi into considerably sharper focus, discovering the hint of something which he intended to examine more closely at his earliest convenience.

The purling curl of the Rio here, though dropped ten feet between mauled banks, was narrower, swifter, or swifter seeming, the southern face scarred and pocked with the unmistakable signs of erosion.

Thoroughly engrossed, Kitchim spent a probing while with glass at eye before abruptly closing and putting it away. The results of this survey occupied his cogitations for such an interval it was very nearly dark when the horse at last clumped him back into town.

Lighted lamps yellowly dappled the road's patterned shadows in front of the shops and strictly adult attractions. Kitchim turned into the first livery he encountered, glad to get down and stamp some feeling into his legs. "Give him the best," he told the gimpy Mexican who came up to take the reins. He paid in advance with a ten-dollar gold piece, waving away the change with a smile. "Where's the best place to eat?"

"Tio Eladio's, patrón. Go with God."

Half buried in the gloom of a dingy alley the place, when tracked down, looked anything but the sort of establishment he was hunting. Its closed plank door, indifferently illumined by a guttering candle in an ancient ship's lantern, looked about as inviting as a basket of snakes. Kitchin, after a single hard scrutiny, pushed it open and stepped watchfully in.

He saw a ratty-looking combination bar and beanery. Check-clothed tables flanked three walls. At the mirrorless bar three steeple-hatted hombres had their heads together. Two lesser men who smelled as though they lived with sheep held down a table with a plate of tortillas, two bowls of steaming chili and a mug apiece of cheap beer.

Kitchim, grimacing, walked on past and dragged out a chair over against the north wall where there weren't any windows to distract his attention. He was, he realized, the only anglo in the place, and wondered what cross-grained impulse had prompted that hostler to send him around to this den of thieves. Ali Baba, he thought, would have felt right at home.

After waiting five minutes without anyone coming to see what he wanted he sent a hard stare at the wizen-faced barkeep and, when that got him nowhere, finally poked up a hand. Getting off his elbows, the fellow, a hunchback, presently shuffled over.

"Your pleasure, *señor*?"

"Grub," Kitchim said. "I'll take whatever you've got ready."

The little gnome, without comment, plodded away, pausing to poke his face through a curtained arch before resuming his stance behind the bar. Kitchim's glance rubbed again across the three conspirators.

Though garbed as vaqueros they looked a pretty ugly lot, particularly the middle one, a big-bellied man burned near as black by the sun as the string-held cloth patch which wholly covered his left eye. The man chose that moment to twist his shoulders and discover Kitchim's regard. Kitchim looked away but felt the man's baleful scrutiny burn across him like a fist.

A black-haired muchacha in a sleazy dress shuffled forward with his meal, Mexican of course and as obviously hot.

As the girl clopped away it seemed the scowling bandido at the bar was leaving also. By stretching his ears Kitchim trapped two words from the departer's admonition to the pair left behind. The first was *quinto* which was Spanish for fifth; the other sounded like *guerras,* but the only connotation he could squeeze from this was that it might be something having to do with a war. With a shrug he choused his thoughts back to the river and, picking up his bone-handled tools, attacked his food.

Finishing, he got up, put a coin beside his plate and, without a further glance toward the pair at the bar, walked across to the door, pulled it open and went out.

A cooler wind was blowing through the

blackness of the alley. Long training in trouble
held him flat against the wall, poised body wholly
still and all the restlessness of his nature funneled
into this grim, prolonged attention, his ears explor-
ing all the sounds of the night. This was what the
years had done to him, it was the price Kitchim
paid for continued survival.

Satisfied he moved, slipping quietly into the
main stream of traffic which, at this early hour,
was easily identified as one skreaking dry-hubbed
wagon wallowing over the ruts of the road, a soli-
tary horsebacker moving toward the lights of the
general store, and a brace of hombres in big hats
and cotton *pantalones* who had just staggered out
of Arristo's, homeward bound, and consoling
themselves with a *pulque*-inspired version of
Jalisco.

They brought back the face of the black-haired
girl and, except for his need to make sure of Fell,
he might have stopped for a drink and whatever
she had going.

He should have been more definite. He could
easily have said, "I'll see you at the stable," but all
he'd put in the note was: "good proposition. El
Federico. June 21."

Been nice to feel you were dealing with a friend,
but fooling himself wasn't one of Kitchim's faults.

Tight-lipped and wary he slipped along through
the dapples of lampshine and shadow, wondering
how he'd locate the man. Fell wouldn't be shouting
his presence from no housetops. He was the care-

fulest gun Jeff had ever run into.

Scanning the shop fronts, one eye peeled for an inn or a flophouse, Kitchim found himself nearing the hitched horse of the man who'd gone into the store.

Pablo Ruiz the sign said. *General Merchandise*.

He could let things rock along, he supposed, and Fell—if he were here—would probably show when and *if* he wanted in. That was one way to play it. But to Jeff's way of thinking there were enough loose ends flapping around in this now.

He reckoned he was going to have to show himself, regardless. He hadn't really wanted Mattie Fell or anyone else, but having offered the guy cards he would prefer to know, before he stacked any chips, whether and how far he dared to count on the man. Fell was bastard enough, if he thought he could cut it, to take over the action. He could be in this store, or in the brush south of town, just grinning and waiting like a goddam spider!

So why, suspecting this, had Jeff got in touch with him?

It was a question Kitchim had asked more than once over the antigodlin miles he had covered getting down here. The answer never varied. He had to have help in a thing big as this. He wouldn't have trusted anyone and Fell with his timidities—his predilection for caution, looked the best bet available.

Jeff had worked with the son of a bitch before and forewarned was forearmed—at least he *hoped* it would work out that way.

He was just preparing to step into the store when a man said behind him, "Like to talk to you a minute."

III

There was a curt civility in the tone, nothing
more.

Every muscle cramping, Kitchim forced himself
to face around with a casualness he hoped might
conceal the urges clamoring inside him.

There was no one on the walk, but through a
door, not six feet away, he met the look of a man
enthroned beside a desk, a balding man grown fat
behind the star that glittered from his shirtfront.

He was not merely big, he was huge, colossal, a
hogshead of a shape with arms like hams and legs
that strained the fullness of his pants, so larded
with flesh as to seem thick as gateposts. Everything
about him was round, his elbows and even the balls
of his knees. The white hair of his beard and the
fringe round his head fluffed like the silk about to
burst from a milkweed and—notwithstanding the

double-barreled gun athwart this caricature's lap—
Jeff's first impulse was to laugh and go on. But that
was before he collided with the stare.

There was nothing about those eyes that looked
humorous. Resettling his stance Kitchim, wiping
the incipient grin off his mouth, growled: "You
talkin' at me?"

The old grafter's look, dropped to Jeff's belted
waistline, came up with a hardening interest.
"Well, well, well!" he wheezed, stare flattering.
"Another pistolero."

Kitchim threw out a look of polite inquiry, striv-
ing behind this—not liking the tone—to hatch up
some story which might reasonably account for a
stranger's presence. It was not helped much by the
crusty inspection digging into his face with the
sharpness of gimlets.

With a rumbling huff that tossed the beard
about his cheeks the badge-toter demanded,
"What's goin' on at the ass-end of nowhere to fetch
s' much trash up outa the bushes? An' never mind
the lies—I've heard 'em all!"

"Why would I lie?" Kitchim said. "Only reason
I'm here is to get across the river. Any law against
that?"

The old hypothecator heaved and gasped like a
boil of lava about to send up a smoke. He got red
in the face, appeared to choke on his fury, but
before he could get his talk box to working a voice
yelled from black depths beyond bars: "Don't
yammer, you fool! *Light a shuck an' git out of
there!*"

While Kitchin stared, stunned, the shotgun moved off its bed of fat just far enough to give Jeff a look down its gullet. Both hammers went back with audible clicks.

The star packer grinned when Kitchim summoned a parched smile. "Caught ye flat-footed, eh? Be smart an' stand still. The mess this thing makes don't hardly bear thinkin' of."

They considered each other through a dragged-out quiet. Weighing Jeff's look, the marshal nodded. "Betsy here's a sure enough caution; you done right t' think twice. I'm Marsh—Oggie Marsh," he said, hugely grinning. "Ain't in no hell-tearin' rush t' git acrosst, be ye?"

Behind frozen cheeks Jeff's mind was jumping like a boxful of crickets. It didn't make sense for Fell to be in this jug but it had been Fell's voice which had yelled that warning.

He said, undecided, "Well, I *had* sort of figured to lay over for the night . . ."

"Come in—come in!" Marsh wheezed, waggling an arm at him.

Kitchim would have preferred to remain where he was but with that cocked Greener balefully ogling his belly it didn't hardly seem as though he had much choice.

Not at all happy he stepped gingerly over the threshold, still wondering about Fell, about what the man's predicament might do to his plans.

Marsh, eyeing him fondly, pawed at his beard. "We got a lot of laws here you mebbe ain't caught up with . . . laws about guns." He paused, eyes bland, a little grin fluttering back the beard from his teeth.

It was Jeff's turn to nod. "But naturally, as marshal, you could look the other way."

"I could tell straight off," Marsh said with approval, "you wasn't no common run of drifter. I'm the J. P. here besides bein' marshal. How much loot you got on you right now?"

Strangling his resentment Kitchim emptied his pockets on the slide Oggie Marsh pulled out from the desk. Coins—gold and silver, a folding knife with two three-inch blades, a stub of pencil and a bullet-bent concha. Fully aware of the marshal's scowl he stepped back.

"What else you got, feller?"

Kitchim, shrugging, spread his arms.

"You *walk* in here?"

"Not quite. I left a wore-out horse at the Bon-Ton Livery, if that's what you're drivin' at. It's howcome I figured to spend the night. I got a brush-scarred saddle and a rifle. An' that's it."

"Fifty-four forty!" Marsh's eyes, adding coins, thinned down to a gimlet stare. "You tryin' t' buy a lawman with peanuts, boy?"

"Not trying to buy anything. You called me in—"

"That's *your* story. I could tell it some different."

They stared again at each other, Kitchim's eyes bitter, the marshal's skeptical with hidden lights back of them a man couldn't fathom. In a disgruntled rumble thinly tinged with satisfaction he declared: "Court's in session. What handle do you go by?"

Jeff, scowling, said: "Kitchim," but Marsh's look didn't change.

"All right, Kitchim. You been picked up on sev'ral counts. How do you plead—guilty?"

There were a number of things Jeff was minded to say but while he stood glaring, Oggie Marsh, clearing his throat, leaned forward to wheeze: "That jasper you heard right after you come in has had two more weeks spliced onto his hitch. F' talkin' outa turn. You throwin' yerse'f on the mercy of this Court?"

Kitchim, assessing his own plight, nodded.

"Then I'm inclined t' be lenient," the old walloper beamed. "Charge of packin' firearms inside the town limits carries a penalty of fifty dollars or two weeks in the pokey—I take it you ain't hankerin' t' spend no time in jail?"

"Take the fifty," Kitchim said, and disgustedly watched Marsh count out and pocket it. He was moving to pick up the rest of his belongings when this outsized Roy Bean of El Federico set a fat finger down upon the folded knife.

"The charge of carryin' concealed weapons inside town limits is punishable by a fine of fifty dollars, one month at hard labor, or both," he pronounced, reaching up around the grin to gently smooth his fluffy beard.

Jeff could feel the hot blood pounding into his cheeks and, clenching his fists, had half opened his mouth when, remembering Fell, he had the wit to close it.

"You fixin' t' be in contempt of this Court, boy?"

Hanging onto himself Kitchim shook his head.

Marsh pursed pink lips, considered his victim and with a great air of tolerance rather ingeniously declared, "I suppose, bein's you're so anxious t' git acrosst the river—an' in view of your straightened financial condition, it would be a act of Christian fo'ebearance if this Court was t' let you go. Providin' we kin reach a amicable agreement about this here fine . . . ?"

Behind the hard clamp of locked jaws Kitchim nodded.

Marsh's bright little eyes from their ambush of wrinkles appeared to weigh him again. "Truck ye got left on that slide ain't negotiable. Horse," he said in a tentative teasing sort of tone, "from what I been told ain't scarcely wo'th more'n thirty . . . guess the Court could allow ye fifteen. How says the pris'ner? Speak up, boy!"

"Done," Kitchim growled.

"Bridle, saddle, blanket an' rifle would mebbe fetch twenty-five—if a man had ary use fer 'em, that is. Considerin' theah condition Court'll hold 'em at ten an' no hard feelin's. You figgerin' t' balk?"

"Afraid that's a luxury I can't afford."

The old grafter chuckled. "Glad ye see which side of the bread gits the butter. Now let's see what we got. Totin' up I reckon we've took care of half of it."

Like some great fat toad in his tiny puddle Oggie Marsh reared back on his homebuilt armless throne of a chair as though, by God, he was maharaja of Hindustani.

Kitchim trembled with rage.

Marsh, grinning, waggled the shotgun. "You wanta throw in that shell belt an' pistol?"

Kitchin, glaring, stood silent and seething, bitterly aware the way this was going he had no more choice than a hooded falcon. No man in his fix could beat a cocked Greener. He snarled in frustration. "I can see you're bound to hogtie me, regardless—how long am I in for?"

Marsh clucked over him like a mother hen. "This Court," he wheezed, "is partial but fair, seekin' on'y t' carry out the letter of the law. Mistuh Kitchim, suh, you're not in—yet." Sighing, the old reprobate declared, "Just t' prove this Court's not unmindful we'll give ye the benefit of the 'warlike intentions' charge—an' if that ain't bendin' over back'ards I don't know what is. Knocks a full ten dollahs off yo' fine. Court'll take belt an' pistol f' the rest of yo' obligation—just pitch 'em on the desk an' ye kin walk right out."

Suspecting a trap, afraid the man's blithe heartiness was no more than front for some cruel trick, Kitchim peered hard at that mountain of flesh before, with fingers he could not quite keep from fumbling, he unbuckled the rig and with considerable reluctance tossed it onto the desk.

Someway managing to keep his lip buttoned he was wheeling to go—was actually in mid turn—when Marsh's hateful voice, reaching whispery after him, inquired spider soft, "Ain't ye about t' be fergettin' somewhat?"

Lividly—speaking through clenched teeth—Kitchim said, "You're expecting *thanks*?"

"Wouldn't know what t' do with it—or them," Marsh replied, flapping a hand at the belongings still littering the desk's pulled-out slide.

IV

Jeff Kitchim stepped into the lamp splashed
street feeling like a skinned rabbit and so buffaloed
and wild he could not have hit the ground with his
hat in three throws.

In a towering rage he struck off for the place
where he'd put up his mount, thinking no further
than to get on him and go, ringy and blind enough
to lash out at anything. But inside half a block the
churn of his passions had sufficiently eased that he
could see the foolhardiness of trying to get away
with a horse the law had confiscated. It could very
well be what Marsh was hoping he'd attempt.

Considering Fell's plight it seemed not unreasonable to suppose El Federico's enterprising
marshal might have a standing arrangement with
the livery's proprietor to pass along the word
whenever a stranger tried to bail out his horse.

Opening his fist Kitchim glared at the slither of coins on his palm, the grubby stub of pencil and the bullet-bent concha which was all Marsh had given him the leave to walk out with. He was minded to pitch the whole works into the street but, glowering, dropped the change into his pocket and, finding himself in plain sight of Arristo's, went catty-cornering over to see what inspiration might be dredged up out of a bottle.

Without a gun he felt naked as a jaybird, all his customary coolness completely out of reach, that experienced cleverness of knowhow and tact as remote to present need as though by God he'd never been in a bind!

And he hadn't—not like this one, vulnerable as a kid in three-cornered pants. Someway he had to get hold of a gun!

It was the only coherent thought he had time for as he moved through the room's smoky light toward the bar. A swarthy long-haired character in cotton pantalones was off in one corner teasing a guitar; the place, even at this early hour, had a pretty fair sprinkling of customers mainly, it appeared, of the boot and saddle variety. And here, again, it seemed he was the only person likely to be considered a *gringo*.

Several wenches with trays were flitting about in their swivel-hipped fashion among the clots of steeple-hatted males as Kitchim, hugging his bottle, pushed away from the mahogany. He was elbowing his way toward a vacant table when his scowling glance chanced to light on a face he had all but forgotten in the same bold interest he'd observed in her before.

Kitchim stared. The girl's red lips pulled away from her teeth and he was hooked, moving toward her, all else discarded in the electric impulse which drew him unthinkingly as flame draws a moth.

She was younger than he'd thought, the discovery almost stopping him until, reassessing the quality of her regard, it became pretty obvious she was inviting his attention, wanting him to come over—daring him to try his luck. He forgot all about the turn it had taken in the urge of old hungers.

Gypsy or Mexicana her features, though fine, were too boldly fashioned for the current trend in beauty. She had, despite her astonishing slimness, all the right curves provocatively distributed, but these were only a part of her appeal, having little to do with the irresistible compulsion that was hauling him nearer. Rather, he thought, trying to settle it later, it was the eyes that grabbed him, something glimpsed in their brightening depths—more challenge than promise, that fetched him across the room to her side.

Not until he'd come up to the table, still peering, half scowling in his trancelike absorption, did he realize what he might be blundering into. The girl was not alone—she had a lot of man with her, the big-bellied ruffian with the black-patched left eye who'd been talking with the pair at the bar in Tio Eladio's, the place where Kitchim had taken his supper. This bull-chested fellow was not pleased to find himself sharing her attention with a strange and boorish *norteamericano*. Nor was he at all adverse to letting Jeff know this. Nor was the girl unaware.

"Pobrecito," she sighed, gaze intent, lips stretching. "I'm theenk the great seizer 'as made your acquaintance."

Kitchim ruefully grinned at her allusion to the marshal. "Afraid he has," he admitted, unable in the baleful glare of her companion to find a more suitable reply. While—glance still locked with the girl's—he was trying, the affronted *bandido*, or whatever he was, surged from his kicked-back chair with an oath. A hint of stained teeth showed behind the twists of a bristling mustache.

"Basta—enough!" he cried, fiercely waving Jeff off, hand plunging swiftly to grab at a knife protruding from the sash wrapped about his bulging gut.

There was no time for choices. Kitchim, unarmed, let drive with the bottle. The man staggered back with blood on his face. The girl, in a flutter, shoved Jeff toward a door. *"Vamanos*—go! *Hurry!"* she gasped; and Kitchim, swearing, found himself stumbling through the trash of an alley.

Panting, off balance, pushed by the sudden cold fingers of panic, he floundered perhaps another five strides before the night wind, blowing up from the river with its smells of dank earth, pulled him back from the crumbling edges of folly. Stopped, grimly listening, he scanned his chances, and moved with caution toward the alley's mouth. More than ever he felt the need of a gun. With a gun and a horse he could be gone from this place, hidden deep in the brush till he could think what to do about Mattie Fell. And, of course, Bavinuchi.

He guessed, a little bitterly, he was going to have to steal them, and it came over him the marshal had probably reached the same conclusion—was likely waiting, even now, to catch him in the act.

But the night was filled with risks and if he were not gone before that business in the cantina came to Marsh's ears he would likely end up behind the same bars with Fell. Black Patch wasn't going to forget this, either, and might even turn out to prove more dangerous than Marsh.

There was no good going to the stables for a mount; that was one place certain to be under surveillance. His best chance, it looked like, was to bide his time and snatch one from the tie-rails flanking the shop-fronts.

Muscles bunched, eyes narrowed, Jeff eased into the street, seeing nothing inimical in that first sweeping glance. There was no commotion pouring out of Arristo's, no appearance of excitement anywhere along the street. Drawing a freer breath his quartering stare swiveled over the racks in a widening astonishment. The only horses in sight were bunched, all four of them, tied to the rail in front of Ruiz's Mercantile.

Kitchim didn't like it. It didn't seem natural. It had the smell of a trap.

The feeling of danger rushed all through him, sweat making a dry prickery stinging along his cheeks. Rooted in shadow he heard a dog yap somewhere. Looking longest at the horses he pondered the street with a solemn care while his pulses thumped and wind blew the cloth of his shirt against his chest. He watched a man come out of the store, anchor his purchases, step into a saddle. And he watched that man ride off up the street through a crisscross of lamplight, turn onto the range and jog off, heading north.

Bitterly murmuring, Kitchim saw no other course but try it. If he waited here long enough they'd all be gone. He speared a bleak look at the dark front of Marsh's office and the spurless strike of somebody's heels coming over the walk, bounding back off the shopfronts, pushed him out of his crouch . . . into reluctant, irretrievable motion.

V

Drifting away from the alley—holding to this casual pace while each stretched nerve thrummed its terrified protest—Kitchim, with the drawn blank cheeks of a gambler, cut over the lifting dust of the street.

You might never have guessed what turmoil seethed behind the locked clamp of that rigid mask —the shock and dread, the cold clawing fears, the scheming, discarding, hoping, desperate slab of wildening eyes as, partway across, Oggie Marsh, with his shotgun, stepped into a splash of light from the store to stand, widely grinning, by that rack of hitched horses.

It was too late to run. There was nothing Jeff could do but go on with a growing sharpness to all his angles while the dogged tramp and sullen rasp of spurred boots took him hopelessly into this confrontation.

And so, rocked to a stop, emptyhanded and filled with the spleen of his bitterness: "Marsh," he said, "what've I done now?"

"That kin wait. It ain't s' much what you've done, d'ye see? as it is that my town's bein' prowled by a drifter." Now the piggish eyes gloated. "A vagrant, a bum without money or prospects—"

"Look! All I want is a chance to get out of here!"

"You had a chance, Mistuh. I turned ye loose once. How many hints does a guy like you need?"

Kitchim's fists were so tightly clenched they ached. "All right," he said, "I'll get moving straightaway."

The fat grin nodded. "That's fer sure." The shotgun leveled. "Move into my office."

Sweat stood damply on Kitchim's tipped face and bound in the cloth stretched across hunched shoulders, shining in the creases that rimmed his pinched mouth. Hate boiled in his stare. The marshal hugely enjoyed it.

"Step careful now—march!"

Finding no help for it Kitchim's shoulders dropped. A great breath fell out of him and he was turning to comply when a cool voice called: "*Minuto uno, señors.*"

Jeff stopped in his tracks. He'd no idea where she'd come from but it was her, all right, the black-haired gitana he had left in Arristo's. Scorn thinned the red lips and the arrogant look of her narrowed the marshal's stare to pale slits.

"Now looky here—" he began.

She paid no heed to his bluster. "W'y 'ave you arrest thees man—eh? Tell me that!"

Marsh heaved and huffed, his great face with its fluttery hair turning crimson. "Am I the marshal of this place or ain't I?"

"Thees man—w'y you are putting heem in your juzgado?"

"'Cause he's a bum, that's why! No-good! A vagrant!" Marsh wheezed and huffed as though about to strangle. "A goddam trouble huntin' puffed-up drifter without no visible means of suppo't—"

"Supote? W'at ees that?"

"Means he ain't got no money—no *dinero*! No job!"

"Oh, but 'e 'as!" The girl's eyes laughed above the curl of red lips. "Ees the man of Don Luis. The new pistolero Bavinuchi 'ave hired to keel off the . . . the how you say—t'iefs? w'at 'ave take so much cattles."

The marshal looked like a stabbed baboon.

Disbelief, consternation and a whole miscellany of less readable emotions jostled and stumbled over the man's gaping features.

Kitchim was some astonished himself, hard put to imagine what had fetched her up with such a notion as this, but liking it too as his mind leaped ahead and an outraged conviction winnowed down through the star-packer's flattening stare.

He didn't ask where she'd got this or how she

knew. With his jaw snapping shut and the fluff fan-
ning out about the grip of his mouth like seaweed
caught in a gigantic wave, Oggie Marsh with his
look turned as flat as a wall, wheeled the heaves of
his girth like some harpooned leviathan and went
wallowing off in the direction of his lair.

Kitchim didn't laugh. He didn't even grin with
the thought of that baleful face sinking through
him. Certain as death and taxes was the shivery
hunch that Marsh wasn't done with him.

The girl touched his arm, brought him back to
the present.

"I'm powerful obliged to you, ma'am," he told
her, and saw the bright lips slide away from her
teeth.

"*De nada*," she said. "Good luck—you 'ave
caballo?"

"Horse?" He shook his head.

"A leetle corral ees behind the cantina. Take the
moro and—*vaya con Dios*." She squeezed his arm
and was gone like smoke in the shadows.

Go with God she had bidden.

With a shake of the head Kitchim let out his
breath and, still pondering her words, cut back
over the street and reentered the alley. Cautious
now with his footing he inched his way through
smashed crates and stacked barrels, testing each
step among the rubble of discarded tins and emptied bottles, still not knowing what to do about
Fell.

He could hardly afford to write the man off.

It didn't seem probable Marsh would keep him

penned long. He would have to be fed. The thinnest slop wasn't free, and from what Jeff had seen the law of this place would have small patience with anything from that side of the ledger. And there'd be hell to pay if Marsh found reason to suspect a connection between his prisoner and the gunhand hired to hunt wolves for Bavinuchi.

That girl was no fool. Leastways there was nothing slow about her wits, coming up slick as slobbers with a windy neat as that. She had sure saved his bacon! Snatched him out of the frying pan cool as you please, and if there was anything back of that yarn she had spun ... What outfit that big didn't lose a few cows? If they were losing enough — Might be just what he needed if he could make them believe it.

He found the pen, and there were two horses in it. He spent five sweaty minutes talking under his breath to them before reaching up to get the hackamore off the horn of the saddle and slide, pulses thumping, between lower bars.

The scarcity of maneuverable space helped considerably. He caught the blue roan without too much fuss and, just to be on the safe side, soon as he'd got the gear piled on he took down the rails and hazed the other horse out. Swinging aboard the blue then he listened, ears stretched, for any hint he'd been discovered. Somebody was still plucking tunes from a guitar but, except for an unexcited murmur of conversation, this was all he could pick up.

It was no time to linger. Eyes wide and quartering Kitchim eased the hide into a carefully held-down walk, moving him into the deeper dark behind buildings. When brush closed around them, Kitchim, breathing a lot freer, pointed the gelding's head toward the river.

In this kind of light it was not too easy to locate a crossing and the best part of an hour slipped away before he found one. Some of this time he spent on his plans, overhauling them somewhat in the light of recent developments. But the girl was never wholly out of his thoughts. He was uncomfortably aware of an undercurrent here, an unwanted premonition that closer acquaintance might prove not only brash but quite possibly downright dangerous. Yet, over and beyond anything he might owe her was the girl herself, turning him unaccountably restless, loosening restraints imposed by cooler judgment.

He tried to hoot away the craziness of notions all too obviously preposterous, laying most of them to abstinence, reminding himself she probably had a dozen lovers and that nothing but trouble could come of seeing her again. He had a stake to make in this country and had damned well better be about it. But the thought of her stayed with him.

He came out of the water perhaps a couple of miles northwest of Bavinuchi headquarters, the frog and cricket chorus thinly bothered in the distance by the barking of a dog. He was clear of Marsh for the moment and had better catch what rest he could; time enough tomorrow to call upon Don Luis.

Night's chill was setting in when he got out of the saddle in a motte of mesquite, hauled the gear off the horse and turned him loose on trailing reins. There was some chance he might lose him but better this, he reckoned, than be caught with a staked-out stolen hide.

He beat the ground with a stick to scare off snakes, gouged a place for his hips and finally stretched out on the sandy earth, covering himself as best he could with the blanket, using the saddle for a pillow.

But his mind kept working, dredging up things far better left lost. The pull of that black-haired witch was working through him and nothing he tried quite put her out of his thoughts. She was still peering at him as, at last, he fell asleep.

The sun was two hours high when the warmth of it woke him.

He threw the blanket aside and got up with the rifle to have his hard look through the stickery branches. Nothing moved in his sight but the horse browsing yonder several hundred yards away.

Even with the riata off its owner's saddle Jeff stalked that coy damned hide clean back to the river before the bastard would step into a loop. Very near wild enough to work the brute over, Kitchim, hand over hank, walked up the rope to stand within feet of that reared-back, ugly, eye-rolling head and all, by God, he could do was glare.

This horse had endured a whole lifetime of hate and had the ridged scars of abuse to prove it. It wasn't just the scars or that stubborn defiance that held Kitchim rigid as something hacked from stone, but the mark, like a skillet of snakes, burned into the left hip—the brand of Bavinuchi.

VI

Evening shadows stretched gray fingers long across the powdery earth when Kitchim, with the heat curling round him like flames, glimpsed again through green branches the hacienda's pink tower. Not, this time, from the direction of the river but from the baked yellow trough of a canyonlike valley which, coming out of the west, lost its crumbling southern wall to become open range as it debouched past the bench housing Bavinuchi's buildings.

It was this which yesterday had so engrossed him while peering through the glass above the Rio's Texas bank, the kind of thing he'd hunted, a bed for raging storm-driven waters. Satisfied now, still aboard the captured roan, he had come to pay his call on Don Luis Capistrano, a gringo astride a stolen Bavinuchi horse.

It got the attention he'd expected.

Through the ferny jade lace of palo verde and huisach he saw the arrested shapes of peons staring in mingled astonishment and fear as, slouched in the saddle, he rode up the lane to stop before the entrance arches and iron-grilled gate, waiting quietly in the quietness. He was a tall man drawn and bony in hunger, sitting a blue horse that did not belong to him with the sweat dripping off his hawk's nose and scarred chin and his half shut eyes bright as cut glass in their insolent survey of the armed guard with spurs and the wolf-faced cur that came sniffling and snarling to circle the legs of this bridleless mount.

"If you value the dog, hombre, get it away from me."

The armed man, scowling, resentfully fingered his antiquated pistol, peered again at the horse, hurriedly crossing himself before he pulled up his jaw in belated remembrance of his authority. "Over there—" he grumbled, spitefully turning to kick at the dog before lifting a pointing hand. "Over there is the place of the man you look for."

"I look for Don Luis."

The fellow stared. "Are you mad?"

"*Por qué?*"

"You think the *patrón* would talk with a gringo?"

"He'll talk with me," Kitchim said, "if he cares for his cows. Look at me, hombre! Go tell what you see—and don't forget the horse."

Dubious, but impressed, the man went into his box and somewhere a bell set up a rusty jangling while Kitchim, considerably less assured than he seemed, embarrassedly listened to the rasp of his breathing. The bell broke into its racket again. A hatless peon came running from a row of mud shacks.

Beckoned inside by the guard they held a muttered conversation, both men several times looking up to scowl through the bars of the box's tiny window. Presently the peon in his cotton pantalones disappeared up a path between trees toward the house.

The guard came out and, with thumbs hooked over the rim of his shell belt, lounged against the plastered mud of his box. Like the sullen yellow eyes of the scrawny dog his roving stare examined a multitude of things while never quite touching the cause of his disquiet.

Kitchim found little humor in the guard's uncomfortable silence. He had his own worries, having thought at some length about the risks he would run riding up to this place on the horse between his legs, accepting those risks because he found no way around them. No one who was anybody in this country ever went anyplace afoot. Besides, with luck, this stolen horse might lend credence to the part. Meekness here held neither promise nor virtue.

Then he saw an old man striding gateward through the splotches of darkening foliage, the peon at his heels awkwardly armed with an arquebus and looking as though at any moment it might bite or explode him into some dreaded hereafter.

Thin and straight, his back like a ramrod, the old man stopped to peer through the gate. Thick gray brows crouched above that bleak stare while the guard straightened into some semblance of attention. "A bold one, this," the old man said, concluding his inspection. A tuft of iron gray hair bristled from his chin and the eyes above that line of clamped mouth revealed nothing. "What do you want?" he said curtly.

"My business is with the *patrón*," Kitchim stated.

"Then speak, man. I am the owner of this place."

"Don Luis?"

"The same."

"And do you make your business the property of the wind to fly where it will across the face of the land?"

The heavy brows drew down in anger. The hacendado coldly smiled, waving his guard and his peon aside. "Did you come here in your effrontery expecting to extort an agreement of pay in return for a promise to stay away from my cattle?"

Kitchin, matching his scorn, said over curled lip, "I can see that kindness has small value here."

"Kindness, *señor*?"

"I considered it a kindness to return a lost horse."

"The horse was stolen. Let us not play—"

"I know nothing of stolen horses, old man. This one I picked up with bridle twenty *kilómetros* south on the road from Laguna Guzman."

"And what made you think it was mine?"

"By the brand—how else?"

Don Luis considered him in skeptical silence, mouth tight with the held-back things he was thinking. "And of course you expected to be paid for your trouble—"

"Only," Kitchim said, "if we came to some arrangement having to do either with the return of your cattle or the apprehension of the persons who have made a business of stealing them."

Something faintly grudging showed in the old man's stare. "Set a thief to catch a thief. Is that your proposition?"

"I've been called worse than that," Kitchim answered, staring down at him. "I don't think it's likely I can get back the cows. I *can* undertake to stop the persons responsible."

"For some pieces of silver you would turn on your own as Judas did Christ?"

"Old man," Kitchim said, "I didn't run off your cattle."

"How did you know I had lost any?"

Kitchim sat a moment regarding him, temper tightening the turn of his mouth. "I'll be taking this horse for my trouble. Good day to you!"

"Anger makes a foul supper. You would not get off this place on that horse—"

"Don't bet on it."

Their eyes clashed and locked. Neither pair pulled away.

The hacendado sighed. "Who hires a thief may wake up a pauper." He grinned, suddenly saying, "Man, what do I call you?"

"My name is Jeff Kitchim."

The old don's eyes held amused disbelief. "No matter," he said, and clapped for his henchmen. "Pablo," he told his peon, "take care of the horse," and, to Kitchim: "Report to the foreman of vaqueros, Jeff."

Kitchim, throwing a leg over the horn, dismounted. He felt the jibe, all right, but he hated to see that rifle get away, yet could hardly protest without diminishing his stature. He had a strong urge to lunge for it when his lifted glance found Capistrano grinning.

Kitchim flushed and stood there, rooted, while the peon led the horse away. He felt the guard's stare, heard the old don chuckle. "Better arm yourself, hombre."

Kitchim said angrily, "You want the men shot?"

"I want them stopped. For this I will pay fifty pesos—each one. How the affair is accomplished is no concern of mine." He turned without further words and strode off through the green blobs of foliage.

The guard went back inside his Turkish bath.

Swearing under his breath Kitchim struck off through the weeds toward the clutter of shacks with his rumbling gut and his hatful of worries. His lack of a weapon was acutely embarrassing but, at least for the moment, he was on Bavinuchi, the man of Don Luis, a hired pistolero entitled to be fed. More, he was where he wanted to be—thanks to the lies told Marsh by that gitana. Maybe the foreman would have a gun he could borrow.

A barefoot girl was quartering over the dust toward one of the hovels as Kitchim emerged, sleeving his face, from the weeds. He called to her. She paused, the brown eyes regarding him with open curiosity, a strange gringo without a gun or horse but with the spurs of a caballero.

"The foreman of vaqueros, *señor? Quien sabe?* Over there ... that is hees house." She stared without comprehension, a look that said, *But aren't all gringo crazy?*

"Who shall I ask for?"

"Teófilo," she said and fled.

Kitchim's glance touched the corrals. They were empty, save for the Bavinuchi roan he'd come in on. He dropped down in the shade and put his back to a post, tipped his hat over his face and took what rest he could.

He awoke in the dark to the racket of horses. Several men, booted and spurred, were noisily hazing them into a pen. He stood up, tiredly stretched, discovering a light in the shack pointed out to him.

Cuffing some of the dust from his pants with his hat, he put it back on and, feeling his hunger, headed for the light.

He knocked and stepped back. Heavy steps

came toward him. The door was hauled open and the foreman stood, a monstrous shape, in the lamp glow.

Kitchim knew at once he'd get no gun from Teófilo. For this—black patch and all—was the man from the cantina he had hit with the bottle.

VII

Many things passed through Kitchim's head in that moment. Recognition was mutual, both sides of the door, nor could there be any doubt of Teófilo's reaction. A tremendous pleasure spilled into his face and this savage satisfaction brimmed the whole look of him as one hand went back to get hold of his knife.

"Wait!" Kitchim cried. "I have orders from Don Luis!"

The man's burning eye never left Kitchim's cheeks nor did the look of it change, but the hand came empty away from his sash. The great chest muscles bulged as he twisted for leverage and the hand blurred out, fisted, to explode in Kitchim's face. And he went flat on his back in the ground's yellow dust.

Desperate, he rolled to avoid chinging boots,

and someway got up onto his feet only to catch another clout that sent him sprawling. Teófilo, grinning, chuckled deep in his throat, hugely waiting while Kitchim, head ringing, got one wobbly knee under him and, finally, gasping, fulcrumed himself into some kind of stance.

The big-bellied walloper's left fist languidly lifted and Kitchim, twisting to duck, took a right across the mouth that spun him halfway round. He backed off, shaking his head, and glimpsed the ring of dark shapes, the avid Mexican faces that, hemming him, ruled out any chance of escape.

He was caught without hope in the gun fighter's nightmare, trapped without weapon against a barroom brawler who had everything going for him, reach and know-how, at least forty pounds and a memory which . . . Jeff clenched his teeth. He'd be lucky if this fellow didn't cripple him for life.

The big Mexican was a quicker man than Kitchim. Despite the belly, Teofilo's ability was evident and the grins of the watchers held no doubt of the outcome. He struck Kitchim twice on the head and laughed as the American went staggering around like a blinded calf. "*Mirar, gringo!*" A flying fist took Jeff in the chest and flung him backward against the massed men. With yells and shouts they threw him back into the man, sledging hard as he could at the foreman's thick middle.

It was like beating a drum and did no good at all. Someone gasped and the world became a pinwheel of lights and Kitchim's knees turned to water. All the breath whooshed out of him and, before he

could fall, there was a kind of hard tug, all motion
reversed and his jerked-open eyes found him
stretched at arms' length above Teófilo's head. The
foreman, turning, put him into a twirl—faster,
faster, and then he spun through the air. He heard
someone dimly give out a great cry, and found
himself floating down a black spiral that appeared
to have no discoverable end.

It was the darkest, weirdest night he could remember, and the longest, most uncomfortable one.
Through all those strange hours unrelenting devils
kept assiduously at him, prodding and rolling,
wrapping and unwrapping, cutting and tieing, as
though he were a bundle being readied for Christ-
mas, all the time talking some outlandish gib-
berish, freezing him, roasting him, ignoring his
pleas, deaf to his curses—doing in fact about everything imaginable to keep him from getting the rest
he needed. And the lights! By God there must have
been two hundred of them, hovering about like a
gang of poor relations at the reading of a will!

He got it doped out that most of the time he had
probably been dreaming, maybe delirious a little.
The first thing he knew for sure he was on his back
in a rope-sprung bunk on a pile of scratchy
blankets framed by four gypsumed walls and
mighty little else. Drunk! he thought, drifting off
again. He seemed to have an impression of soft
cool hands passing over his face.

The next time the white walls floated into focus,
his quickened glance took in the window, a tiny,

many-paned affair through which a hot wind was blowing from a day that was just about shot.

Struggling onto an elbow he discovered he was naked, and his mind groped to grasp what hotel he'd gone to bed in—a pretty crummy place he decided, peering about. Then his glance found his clothes, all washed and clean again, on a packing crate over at one corner. More mystified still Kitchim flung off the blanket to swing feet to floor —a *dirt* floor, by God!—and that was when the pain hit, oozing from every joint. He braced himself, gasping, all the bones in his body feeling like they'd been poleaxed; and he fell back, groaning, in the shake of a sudden chill.

The place was gray with shadows when, gingerly, he managed to push up again and, panting, chanced a look at himself, staring in clammy wonder. That hadn't been all dreams and delirium. Someone had sure as hell worked him over, and they hadn't missed much. From neck to knees he was purple-green splotched with a profusion of bruises he was open-jawed eyeing when something tugged his glance to the door.

It stood widely ajar, blocked by a shape whose beefy face brought everything back like a drench of cold water.

Teófilo said, "Tomorrow you work or get off thees ranch."

Kitchim worked. From dawn till dark in a dreary succession of interminable hours he wrapped up every bastardly chore the man threw at him, hatefully, bitterly biding his time. He had no idea what had happened to Fell. He could still be in jail or gone from the country; Jeff had no way of knowing and scant time for wonder. Teófilo delighted in finding the roughest, most danger-fraught jobs for him, and always there was someone keeping tabs. Never was he left unwatched for more than a handful of minutes—not even at night. This surveillance chafed like a saddle sore, the more since any pay he might earn must derive entirely—under the terms of his presence—from the apprehension or killing of cow thieves. Apparently in ignorance the foreman left him no time for poking around. Only one good thing, aside from toughening him up, had come out of his plethora of back-breaking peonage. A working grasp of Bavinuchi geography and, to a lesser extent, some idea of the deployment of riders.

Four days passed in this frustrating itinerary, Kitchim eating with the unmarried cowboys in a kind of barracks-like mess hall a stone's throw south of the pink-towered chapel. Turning out of the place now with Domatilio Vargas, the close-mouthed man assigned by the foreman to share quarters with him, Jeff was warily astonished to find Teófilo waiting.

The boss vaquero wasted no words. "You are wanted at the house, hombre, *Andale! Pronto!*"

Passed through the gate, discouragedly wondering if Don Luis expected a progress report, Kitchim approached the massive shape of the hacienda's big house, feeling a wind coming up off the desert, hearing the cottonwoods rustle

overhead, seeing the dark shapes of the *tabacón*
eaves, keeping to the gravel. He came up to the
front and swung around on the flower-bordered
path that led off to the side and a proper entrance
for peons, paid help and others not socially accep-
table, and then said, "To hell with it!" and, going
back to the portal, pounded on the door.

It was opened at once and by their expressions it
would have been difficult to say which was the
more astounded, Kitchim or the girl who stood
framed in the opening.

She looked breathlessly frightened and Jeff,
shaken too, imagined for a second he was out of his
head again. He couldn't help gaping. Black of hair
as that snake-hipped witch of Arristo's cantina . . .
white teeth too, same color of eyes. But that one's
eyes had been bold and inviting as the lure of red
lips and off-shoulder blouse which had taken him
into that clash with Teófilo.

This was a girl raised for better things whose real bearing, rich dress and shocked stare spoke of
blood so blue it could have no acquaintance with
brown bottles and bars and the other wild things
which connected her up in Jeff's mind with the girl
who had talked him out of Marsh's clutches.

Confused, taken aback, he dragged the hat off
his head like the rest of the paisanos when con-
fronted by one of the dons or their women; and
then, flushed in resentment, was opening his mouth
when, with hand at throat, she cried, "Why are you
here?"

Kitchim suddenly grinned. "You do not recog-

nize the man of Don Luis? The paid pistolero—"
"You fool!" she whispered. "Get out!"

VIII

Kitchim, turned stubborn, stepped inside and, grimly considering her, shoved the door shut. "I don't know what kind of game you're playing but it's plain enough you wanted me here—"

"I did not send for you! *Madre de Dios,* do you think I am *loco*?"

"In town . . . " he began, but she stormed through his words breathing scorn and fury. "In the town ees not here! Do you imagine my father—"

All I know is Teófilo said I was wanted at the house."

"Teófilo . . . ? Does he know," she said quickly, "you are here about the cows?"

Kitchim shrugged. "Don Luis may have told him. He don't know it from me."

She stood there chewing her lip, lost in thought.

He said, "What difference?" and then remembered the surveillance, how filled with work his days had been.

"I asked for a rider." Her tone was worried. She raked him with a searching stare. "Why would he send *you*?"

"I'm a rider."

She considered him doubtfully, lip caught in teeth again, a remote speculation stirring back of her eyes. She said, "You don't understand . . ." then pushed it away from her. "It's my father." Fright came into the dark search of her glance. "He needs a doctor."

"What's the matter with him?"

"His side, I think. He talks . . . different—he can't use his right arm."

Stroke, Kitchim thought, and narrowed his eyes at her.

She said, breathless, "El Federico."

Jeff got the message. Marsh, of course; she was bothered by what the marshal might do to him. But Marsh, first of all, would have to lay hands on him, and Kitchim had no intention of repeating the blunders which had trapped him before. "Chances are he won't. . . . Where do I look for this pillroller?"

She gave him directions, said nervously: "Wait—" and came back with a pistol, a single shot .50 caliber pocket gun, a weapon much in vogue among the gambling fraternity. "Take this," she said, pressing it into his hand, "and—be careful."

He should have gone at once but, slipping the belly gun into a pocket, he kept hold of her hand. With the smell of her hair unsettling his thinking and the wide searching eyes of her so darkly there just in front of his own, the crazy notions set loose got through his guard and he pulled her against him.

"Please . . . " she gasped. "Don't . . . " but he smothered her struggles, pursued the twist of her cheeks until her mouth, finally captured, lay under his own. She quit squirming then and Jeff, finding no resistance, kissed her again, and once more for good measure. Turning loose of her then with a satisfied grumble he yanked open the door and plunged into the night.

At the pens he roped out a dark bay without blaze, tossed a blanket across it and was just cinching up when Teófilo's spindly shanks and burly shoulders came out of the dark with a challenging "*Quien es?*"

"Kitchim," Jeff said.

"What are you doing with that horse?" the man asked in Spanish.

"I'm off to El Federico."

"At whose orders?"

"The *patrón's.*"

The foreman of vaqueros, completely still, regarded him. "What does he want?"

"*Un medico.*"

Teófilo, sounding suspicious, said, "For whom?"

"He did not confide in me." Jeff picked up the reins and the big foreman, grudgingly, allowed him to pass.

Kitchim led the horse out and swung into the saddle, feeling the stab of Teófilo's regard. But all the man said was, "Make a quick trip of it and don't lose that horse."

Kitchim pointed the bay toward the river. Now, by God, he'd find out a few things! Then he thought of the girl and patted his pocket. A don's daughter. "Damn!" he said, remembering the feel of her. But, crossing the river, more important considerations took hold of him, and the look of Marsh's eyes, flat and shiny as fish scales, stirred an increasing uneasiness in him.

Understanding border politics he could find more sense in the marshal's turning loose of him, now that he knew the girl was Don Luis' daughter. Just the same, he reckoned, he'd be wise to get the doc and recross the Rio soon as possible.

But there was Fell to consider, the man's part in Jeff's own plans, the scheme which had fetched Kitchim into this business. He had not given up the notion, was more set in it than ever, and a few ideas had turned up during the days he'd spent as Teófilo's private peon.

Yet he still felt the burning need for a gun— something more than the toy in his pocket which he considered to be worthless beyond ten feet. Something with more than one load in the barrel, something that would stop a man beyond the range of Marsh's Greener. Nor was Kitchim forgetting that Bavinuchi foreman.

Kitchim thought—everything considered—Teófilo had been just a little too restrained this evening. Almost as though, behind the gruff tone, things were falling into place in a way that secretly pleased him . . . and the girl had said she had *not* asked for him but only for a rider.

Why had Kitchim been picked?—a man Teófilo had been watching like a hawk? Had there been more to that beating than a blow from a bottle? Had the foreman found out or someway guessed the reason this gringo was riding for Bavinuchi? The girl had voiced that thought, too. Had the boss vaquero smugly imagined he had just said good-by to a dead man?

There was food here for thought and Kitchim, leaving the bay to pick its own gait, chewed and rechewed it with increasing disquiet. He recalled the unsavory pair he had seen with the foreman in the bar at Tio Eladio's—that talk of *quinto* and *guerras,* and wondered what day of the month this was. Wondered, too, if there were any connection between Teofilo and El Federico's gargantuan badge-packer. And while his suspicions were traveling apace Jeff asked himself also what the daughter of Don Luis—garbed and be-baubled like a girl of the Ursari Bear Tamers—had been doing hanging around Arristo's cantina. It would bear looking into, he was sure enough of that.

But with the gun-slinging brethren first things

came first, and only a fool ever looked behind. One way or another a man's mistakes were mostly written off in gunsmoke—as Jeff's could be were he to figure this wrong.

Eyeing the lights of the town he decided first of all to get hold of another gun; time enough then to go look for that sawbones. And if the old man worsened it was no skin off *his* nose. Might be better all around so far as Jeff was concerned. Bavinuchi might be up for grabs, and with an unmarried daughter . . .

Kitchim smiled a slow smile and turned his attention to conning the night. The girl he could handle. He had better make sure he could take care of Marsh.

Two sources of guns, both risky, were available. The rack at Arristo's where men hung up their weapons in accordance with Oggie's ordinance. And the mercantile which, if closed, he could burgle.

Under other conditions he would have chosen the latter, but it was cheek by jowl with the marshal's office, so he cut off through the brush to come up behind Arristo's.

No mounts had been left in the little pen tonight. Swinging down Kitchim snubbed his Bavinuchi horse to one of the poles, securing the reins with a slipknot on the off-chance he might care to leave in a hurry. Ignoring the door he had departed by, remembering the rack had been against the front wall, he worked his way through the alley's trash, stepped up onto the walk and lounged against the dive's front while narrowed eyes went skittering through the street's blue-black shadows.

Nothing untoward there. The mercantile was dark but light splashed the walk in front of Marsh's office. If there *was* any connection between Marsh and Teófilo, or if the foreman had sent Oggie word that Jeff was coming, nothing Jeff could see gave this any support. If the mercantile's darkness was in aid of a trap Kitchim wished Oggie joy of it and, pushing open the door, stepped into the cantina.

Six or seven steeple-hatted drinkers were holding down the bar with perhaps that many more scattered around among the tables, and off at one corner the long-haired kid in the cotton pantalones was singing of unrequited love while mauling the strings of his homemade guitar. Jeff did not notice any significant attention.

With an appearance of nonchalance he paused by the rack, face settling into a tighter clamp when, looking them over, the only thing he saw even relatively modern was an indifferently cared-for single-action .44 holstered to a battered belt whose loops held less than half their complement of cartridges. Reaching for this he heard the door open back of him, could feel the harsh stab of the newcomer's stare.

It was too late to get any good out of turning. He clapped the belt round him, jerking the tongue through its big silver buckle, carrying himself in three strides against those fellows at the bar who stood, eyes sprung with horror, watching over his shoulder the loom of catastrophe.

"Hei, Pito!" rang the marshal's high yell. "Grab him—*grab him*!"

And a man's chin came round, one of the pair Jeff had seen with Teófilo. But this chap, with Jeff's pocket pistol ready to take his everlasting picture, wasn't grabbing anything.

IX

This, when the chips were down, was one who could think. As Jeff brushed past, bound for the door he had left by before, near the bar's far end, the fellow thrust forth a foot.

It threw Kitchim hard but he kept hold of his pocket gun and, as three others dived for him, fired point blank. One man, twisting in mid-air, screamed. The others, eyes enormous, went stiff in their tracks as Jeff, bounding up, slashed back a hand for the stolen pistol.

It was gone from the holster, spilled in his fall. "Bavinuchi!" he yelled, and threw the empty pocket gun across the room in a glittering streak just as the marshal was bringing up his Greener.

The shotgun roared but Jeff was down, scooping up the pistol, careening round the bar. The place was a bedlam as he crashed through the door.

Outside, the night wind cold against his streaming cheeks, jerking loose the reins he got a foot in the stirrup and, oblivious to racket, had the horse in a hard run before he touched saddle.

Straight south he rode, pounding loud for the river, the bay's ears flat to the sides of his head. Not till the brush closed round them did Kitchim slow, and not even then for another five minutes of branch-popping progress. He wanted no doubt about where he had gone, for the moon was up now and he must still return to get hold of that pillroller. And more important than this—to Jeff's way of thinking—was the honed-sharp need to know what day of the month this was. He could not leave that lay with the foreman, Teófilo, grown so large in his mind.

When he picked up the shine of the river he swung west along the near crumbly bank, glance lifted, hunting with sweat-stung eyes for a crossing; turning back, when he found one, in a northerly quartering; walking the horse, all his senses alert; seeing the shape that rose out of blue shadows, throwing his gun on it, holding the hammer ready under his thumb. "Careful, now! Watch it!"

"That you, Kit?"

It was Fell with both arms stiffened over his head.

Jeff pulled up, staring down at him. "Marsh turn you loose?"

"Three days ago." Fell, lowering his arms, began a bitter cursing. "No gun, no horse, no goddam money—"

"You'll have money 'fore we're done with this."

"It better be plenty. If you could seen the slop that sonvabitch fed—an' not a mouthful since but three-four gophers! Goddam gut thinks my throat's been cut! I owe you a lot, man."

Kitchim, eyeing that glowering face, said, "What day's this—what day of the month?"

"Who cares . . . ?" Fell began, said gruffly: "Fourth."

"*Guerras* ring any bells with you?"

Fell's gangling frame quit its restive flutter. The bony shoulders tipped, the narrow chin came up to show this staring, his grumbling voice, softer now, said, "Up the river a piece there's a town of that name. I come through gettin' down here—"

"How far?" Jeff said.

"Ten mile, mebbe. What's Guerras to do with us? That where this dough is hid?"

Kitchim explained his deal with Don Luis, then told of seeing Teófilo and those other two at the bar that night in Tio Eladio's. "I caught two words, *quinto* and *guerras*—"

"An' come up with it's this foreman that's liftin' the cows, eh?" It was plain Jeff's companion was a long way from sold on it. "You pull me here for a two-bit play?"

"I don't know what Teófilo's up to—revolution, maybe, but he's sure up to something and better be stopped if your idea in coming was to leave with full pockets. It's Bavinuchi—place he's foreman of —that I've got my eyes on."

"Your eyes, eh? What's that supposed t' mean?"

"Means I expect to take over—"

Fell's bitter laughter cut him off. "Bavinuchi? What kinda stuff you been smokin'? Bavinuchi!" he snorted. "Why'n't you jest figger to lop off Chihuahua!"

Kitchim lifted the reins. "It's no job for weak hearts." He kneed the bay into motion.

"Here," Fell growled. "Wait!" and caught hold of the stirrup. "Never said I . . ."

Kitchum, stopping the horse, grimly eyed him. The man looked what he was, a tiger-faced Texan who got his living with a gun and was good enough with it to command top pay. But there were plenty of others and Jeff, rubbed wrong, brought this fact to Fell's attention. "I could have passed the word to Beal, or Carrondaga; I could name an even dozen who'd have jumped at the chance to partner the man who grabs Bavinuchi. Nobody's forcing you."

"Hell, I'm in. It's just . . . a man likes t' know where he stands . . . Bavinuchi's *big*. How can two guys—?"

"You know what a banco is? Ever read the treaty our rough-ridin' Teddy cooked up with Mexico? Provides that whenever, wherever, a chunk of land, big or little, is lopped off either the U.S. or Mexico by reason of the Rio Grande changing its bed, that chunk shall henceforth be a part of the country on whose side of the river the new channel leaves it. Which is how El Federico comes to be a part of Texas—savvy?"

Mattie Fell broke suddenly out of his tracks,

eyes stretched wide, the whole look of him incredulous. "You think Bavinuchi's goin' to jump
them banks?"

"With an assist from us—with a little help—
yes."

Fell shook his head. "I git out from under my
hat to your gall."

"Well? You in it or ain't you?"

Fell, narrowing his eyes, let the stillness run,
scowling at the concept, rasping the palms of his
pretty hands together, irritably growling as one
then another of the risks caught his notice. "How
we gettin' past the rest of it—even if the river de-
cides t' do what we want? Damn little of that stuff
in El Federico—"

"The worrying is *my* job. All I need from you is
a kind of touchy help, and I haven't got the time to
argue about it now. Yes or no?"

Fell, uneasily frowning and —like Jeff before
him—still woolling it around the darker corners of
his mind, was unable to resist the picture painted
by cupidity. "Yes . . . " he said and, skewered by
Kitchim's stare, finally pulled his mouth together.

Kitchim watched him a moment longer. "You
can drop out of this right now and no hard feelings—"

"Said I was with you, didn't I?"

"All right," Jeff said, describing the hard-faced
pair who'd put their heads with Teófilo's by the bar
where he'd first seen them—Pito and the other.
"Arm yourself and get over to Guerras. See if you
can locate one or both of them; just find them and

sit tight. I'll see you there tomorrow. Be around
and be ready."

He touched the horse with his spurs.

He was moving at a walk when he came in behind the town's mostly dark buildings and quit the
saddle to stand deep in silence a hundred yards
back of the doctor's mud house, thinking mostly of
Fell while he listened to the night and lengthily
considered the immediate surroundings. The wind
had dropped but there were no crickets chirping.
The quiet breathed over his nerves like they were
harp strings. Farther back, under tamarisks at the
townward end of the house, something moved.

Looked as black, off there, as India ink. No
gleam of lamp came through the doctor's windows;
only way to make sure was go up there and knock.
There were several notions scriggling around behind Jeff's stare, but setting up a mark for Marsh's
Greener wasn't one of them.

Something told him to stay away from there.

He could go back of course and claim the doc
had been out of town. The girl would have no way
. . . but that damned foreman might! He may had
ridden in himself hoping to catch Jeff in something
he could use to be rid of him. He might have sent
another hand. He might have let Marsh know Jeff
was coming across the river, but the marshal
hadn't known he would flush Jeff when he stepped
into Arristo's or he'd have made a better job of it.

A man could speculate all night and never butter
any parsnips.

Kitchim could feel the run of sweat across his

cheeks. His mouth turned small and grim as his
glance reached again across the moon-blued shadows, appraising that deeper dark beneath the trees.
If a man was over there—if it weren't just some
strayed cat or prowling dog it could as well be Fell
as anybody else.

Jeff hadn't mentioned the sick don or told Fell
where he was bound for, but this·did not preclude
his having learned from other sources. He had only
Fell's word for it the man didn't have a horse.

Kitchim cocked the gun he had taken from the
cantina and, fed-up with waiting, started carefully
toward the house.

X

Hung over the town in argent splendor the lopsided moon seemed bright enough to read by. Away from the horse, caught full in its glare, he had almost reached the point he aimed at when the rhythmic scrape of shovel against earth sent him into a spread-toed, frozen crouch.

Who in the name of Job's lost ox would be outside digging at this damned hour?

The sinister rasp of it was almost certainly emanating from some place beyond that westernmost wall—the town end where tree gloom was deepest . . . about where he'd thought to have glimpsed something move.

He couldn't think why the steady slither and tump of this clandestine shoveling should bring into his mind the black-patched face of the burly foreman but it was there, darkly smiling in the oddly pleased look that was the last Jeff had seen of him. He remembered the girl's "Does he know you are here about the cows?"

Kitchim, growling, was against the house when he happened to recall it was Marsh she'd looked afraid of, and he wondered again what she'd been doing at Arristo's. He made a twist in his thinking to ask about that and then, spider soft, he was rounding the corner, staring, scarce breathing, through a swirl of stirred shadows at the bent, blacker shape leaning over the shovel.

"Strike a light," Kitchim spoke, gun leveled from the hip.

Without flurry the man slowly pushed himself erect. "I can see—"

"Strike a light!"

With a sigh the man reached into his discarded coat, got a lucifer block from a pocket and scratched one.

Kitchim softly swore. Whatever he'd imagined he would find it wasn't this. The fellow—a man Jeff had never before encountered—had been setting out what looked to be rose cuttings and tulip bulbs. "Kind of funny time—" Kitchim began. The fellow snorted. "Man in my line of work's lucky to find *any* time! What with buryin's and birthin's . . . "

"If you're the doc," Kitchim said, "you're wanted at Bavinuchi."

The old fellow, grumbling, picked up his coat.

"Ain't no one chopped off his tassel has he?"

"It's Don Luis. From what the girl said I expect he's had a stroke."

"Been courtin' one long enough." Doc twisted his head. "Don't seem to remember comin' across you before."

Kitchim shrugged. He put the pistol away. El Federico's pill man said, "How'd it effect him?"

"Well, she said—"

"*Who* said?"

"The girl—"

"Some of 'em, maybe, ain't got a pot to piss in but they've all got names, an' there's half a hundred of 'em—which are you talkin' about?"

"Capistrano girl."

"Daughter, eh?" Jeff could feel his eyes sharpen. "She's got one—Meetah. Prob'ly comes from the Spanish; Amita, I'd guess." Held by a finger he had the coat over a shoulder, leaning on the shovel while he toted Jeff up and couldn't seem to be satisfied.

"What's the chances," Kitchim asked, "of His Nibs kicking the bucket while we're lallygaggin round here shooting the breeze?"

Tossing the shovel aside, nodding, Doc said, "You do have kind of a pins-and-needles look. Prob'ly need more greens in your diet. Can he move everythin'?"

"My job's cows. Girl says he talks funny, having some trouble with one of his arms."

Doctor stared a breath longer, bobbed his head again, clucking. "No rush I'd say. You'll find ol'

Frannie in the shed off yonder. Get a saddle on her, will you? I'll fetch my bag."

At Bavinuchi the guard passed them through without comment. The moon had moved over some. It must have been about three but there was light in the house. A moza opened the door before Jeff could knock and took them gray-faced through a shrub-prettied patio to call at a door off a flower-banked gallery which Meetah threw open to beckon in the doc.

The servant withdrew and Kitchim, left to himself, strode about for a bit, hardly noticing what he looked at, winding up finally staring into a fountain bubbling out of piled rocks and cattail-like growth behind a drinking iron deer and a pair of cast ducks.

He found his thoughts clumsily jumbled. Why had the marshal turned Fell loose? To cut expenses? Cut his losses? Or as decoy for some kind of fishing expedition? A wily bird, that Marsh, a grafter sure, but a deep one, a sharp one with a nose honed for profit. Had he already sniffed a connection between them and turned Mattie loose to prove his suspicions? Had he only just happened to step into Arristo's when Jeff had been lifting that gun from the rack? Had he been told to expect Jeff, warned perhaps by Teófilo?

It seemed plain as plowed ground the Bavinuchi foreman was up to something, certainly. Tomorrow at Guerras, if Fell did his part, they might have a few answers Jeff could use to better his standing,

perhaps even to institute himself here permanently
—or for as long, anyway, as it suited his purpose.

There was a shorter route he could take he
thought sourly. He hadn't known about the girl
when he had first shaped his plans. He wasn't
partial to double harness—had been lone-wolfing
it too long, he reckoned; but marriage would certainly improve his position—might even dispense
with his need for Mattie Fell, whom he trusted
even less than he could this don's daughter.

He turned at her step. She looked troubled in the
starshine and stopped beyond reach to stand in silent appraisal, watchfully weighing him, reminded
no doubt of his proclivities and strength. He
grinned at her, wryly. "The bad penny returns—
didn't you think I would, Meetah?"

"Where did you get the belt and pistol?"

"What were you doing at Arristo's that day?"

Her tongue went over dark lips thoughtfully. "A
trade?"

"Why not? The hardware came from the rack in
Arristo's."

"You just helped yourself? No one objected?"

"It got a little sticky but I got clear in one piece."
He told her about it, briefly stating the facts."
" 'Fraid I lost your artillery."

She shrugged this aside, continuing to eye him
with that dark speculation stirring again across her
cheeks. The doc, coming out of her father's room,
approached them. Seen more clearly he was big
shouldered, bandy-legged, better suiting the role of
country deacon in his lifeless black, pale shirt and

dark tie. He stopped with chin lowered, studying them from under shaggy brows. Hatless now, head gleaming in its baldness, he showed a broad nose, mouth wide lipped but caustic.

"He'll keep until morning. Reckon you'll want me to sleep here—"

"Of course." The girl clapped her hands. "Will his arm . . . ?"

"Depends. Probably I'd say, if there are no complications. That side of him's partly paralyzed, but if we can keep him stationary, keep down excitement, I would think he'd be up and around before long." He considered her for a moment. "Don't suppose you could guess what brought this thing on?"

She looked at him doubtfully.

"He been worryin' about anything?"

"We've been losing some stock."

"Cows? Yes, I see," the doc said, glance swiveling to Kitchim. The moza came up, Meetah explaining his needs, and he followed the girl off, leaving the pair of them alone again. Kitchim said, "And now . . . about Arristo's?"

"I was watching for you."

Kitchim's smile was thin, disbelieving. He shook his head at her.

"It's true," she said, and pulled up her chin. "For someone *like* you, at least. Someone quick with a gun." She said, nervously watching him, "You have learned something, haven't you?"

It was Jeff's turn to shrug. "Bit early to tell—"

"But you have your suspicions?"

"I've got a passel of them. What," Kitchim growled, "took you there the second time—to Arristo's, I mean . . . when I found you at that table?"

"But I've already told you."

"Looking for a gun fighter?" Kitchim narrowed his eyes at her. "How many grab-an'-shoots you figurin' to hire?"

"But how could I know you were going to come over here?"

He considered her look of childish astonishment. "And the gypsy get up—you always wear that when you step down to deal with gringos?"

Even in this blue light he could see the stain of color that pulsed into her cheeks, the tightening mouth, the flat and far-off look she raised between them. "And Teófilo," he said, throwing in the rest of it. "You two looked pretty cozy—"

She slapped his face and stepped back, breathing hard. "I do not have to answer your questions or account for your cheap stupid gringo suspicions!" Indignation burned through her stare, and she whirled in a flutter of skirts and was gone.

XI

Finally done with scowling after her, Kitchim let himself out and returned to the mud box in which he shared sleeping space with Domatilio Vargas, the bird dog Teófilo had detailed to keep tabs on him. The bunks were built one above the other and both of them were empty when Jeff, shedding clothes, climbed into the upper.

Bone weary, he expected sleep to elude him. Too many things were spinning round through his thoughts, suspicions and worries for which he had no sure answers. He seemed each year to tire quicker, come back slower and take less joy in the things he did. This was part, he guessed, of the same harsh truths which had fathered the conviction that he had to make it now if he would make it at all. Bavinuchi, if it didn't take care of him, could damn well be his Waterloo.

He woke, filled with aches from his twisting and turning, to a room black as soot, crammed with a kind of listening stealth that had frightened away all the insect sounds and left in their place a kind of pulsing dread that could only come from the nervous stab of unseen eyes.

With a straining care—not otherwise moving—he felt around for the pistol he had got into bed with. As his hand closed upon it—as he was bracing himself to throw off the blanket—the jerk and rasp of the nerved-up breathing grew still then bounced into a jumpety off-key whisper. "*Jefe!*"

Kitchim, swinging both legs over the side, snarled, "For Chrissake! Ain't you no better sens'n to come in here?"

He could see her now against the thinning gray of the slot-like window built in without glass. "You want to get me shot?" he growled, hugging the blanket and wondering uncomfortably where the hell Vargas was.

"I had to come—there's no one . . . "

"Even the goddam night has *eyes*!"

"It's not night now; in ten minutes it will be daylight." She drew a shuddery breath. "They've gone!"

"Who's gone?"

"The vaqueros . . . the ones, anyway, that were quartered near you."

Kitchim, dropping onto the floor in his blanket, still gripping his gun, peered through the gloom at her, thoughts racing and edgy. "How do you know?"

"I've been watching for this—I heard them! I saw them!"

"How many?"

"Perhaps a dozen . . . It's Teófilo, isn't it?"

"When?" he said.

"Perhaps two hours ago—maybe three. Is Teófilo . . . ?"

"Probably." They'd be heading for Guerras if he had this pegged right, for Guerras with cows. And if Fell didn't spook them . . . "As boss vaquero," he said, thinking aloud, "the guy wouldn't have much trouble laying out work to give the ones with him all the chance they'd need to move and have ready any she-stuff they wanted. All bred, of course." He pulled the chin off his chest. "If they've been making off with any sizeable bunches how come nobody's tracked 'em down?"

"Teófilo has been the one to go after them. Always, he says, the tracks disappear."

Kitchim, nodding said, "They probably do. There'd be some of the men, anyway, he'd have to fool."

"But you think you can find them?"

He wondered at the eager-anxious way she put the question. Man would almost think the purse was hers they'd come tumbling out of. He had closer things to think of, wasn't paying much attention to her gabble. He should have insisted her father put the deal in writing . . . what if the old man decided to renege or, after Jeff had this licked for him, refused to believe his own range boss was guilty?

She put the question again, both tone and look demanding an answer. Kitchim checked the drive of his temper, saying dryly, "It's been generally my habit to do what I set out to—"

"Take me with you," she said, and it hauled him out of his thinking to stare.

The light was good enough now that he could see she had dressed for it. She caught the uncharitable cut of his glance. "If it turns out to be Teófilo," she urged, "you may be glad to have someone to substantiate your side of this. An impartial witness."

He scowled at the inference. But she could very well be right. It wasn't clear to him why he didn't want her with him. There was Fell, of course, the risk of stray bullets . . . the need to take Fell over the ground. He knew these were only excuses. But without going into the thing any deeper it was all too apparent he hadn't much choice. Unless he cared to turn the girl against him.

He concealed his reluctance behind expressed pleasure, sent her off to get saddled while flinging into his clothes. Women! he thought. There were only two kinds. Good ones and bad ones. And this was the knowledge that kept disturbing his judgment, feeling the pull of her, thinking how easily . . . worriedly resenting her ability to unsettle him, knowing he ought either to ignore her completely or bend every effort in the direction of marriage. She could be charmed into it. Hadn't spurned his kisses had she? A masterful man was just what she needed.

And such a union, he realized, had everything

going for it, obviating the perils of depending on
Fell, making wholly unnecessary the sweat and
fragile planning required for bancos and changed
channels and the subsequent adjustments which, so
far, he hadn't even gone into. Intimidation, open
belligerence, would be the best answer probably for
any adjusting once the hacienda had been removed
from Mexican jurisdiction.

But adjusting a sick and frail old man was one
thing. Intimidating Meetah, backed by half a hundred reckless vaqueros, could be something else
again; and the first imperative in any event was the
permanent removal of that rogue Teófilo. There'd
be no reconstructing that one.

So—on to Guerras.

But he could see the sense in making it appear
they must rely on tracks—all the trumpery of signs
and signal smokes—if they were to come up with
the robbers' destination.

They set forth in the first rosy tint of dawn.
Meetah had been impatiently awaiting his appearance at the pens with saddled horses and a
bewildered ragtag of six armed peons, bandoleered
and barefoot, shy—even embarrassed, in this un-
precedented situation.

Eyeing them Kitchim almost threw up his hands.
"If we've got to have help," he had growled disgustedly, "why not take some of your *regular*
riders?"

He'd seen her head snap up, the rebellious detail
of darkening cheeks, so he was not too surprised at
the way she lashed back, declaring that in the first

place none of Bavinuchi's regular riders were about
and that, all things considered, nobody with the
wits of a half-grown goat could afford to put any
trust in them anyway unless—in Jeff's wisdom—he
could point out the loyal ones.

Bridling under what he took to be sarcasm,
seething at having to endure this from a chit of a
girl, Kitchim, jerking a nod, went up into leather,
grinding his teeth on the need to snap back, scarcely able in spite of this to keep his lip buttoned.

It was not hard in a tucked-away section of river
bottom to pick up the sign of moved cattle sur-
charged with the marks of shod and ridden horses.
Nor was this difficult to follow through several ob-
lique shifts until, around noon, the pushed cattle
came into a region of malpais, a dark basaltic lava
choking out all vegetation save occasional sparse
clumps of cottony looking bunch grass. This rusty
rocklike covering, sharp in many of its edges and
easily displaced where individual pieces were sufficiently small to turn under the scuff of hoof or
boot, appeared extensive and was, Kitchim knew
from personal experience of the stuff in other
places, hell on beasts and practically impossible to
follow anyone through.

He had no intention of attempting to track either
the robbers or the stolen Bavinuchi cattle across so
desolate a stretch. They'd have a sore-footed herd
in mighty short order if they went for any distance
into this kind of country, nor could he believe
Teófilo would be so foolish. He'd stay with it just
long enough to bury his trail, coming out at some

place easily missed by any who might seek to follow. Jeff, with his chips on Guerras, took a long dreary look at this black chunk of country and—not averse to increasing his stature—waved the peons disgustedly away from it.

He could feel the girl's stare but, giving her never a glance, choused his sweating paisanos off toward the river which, invisible from here, ran almost at right angles to the apparent direction being taken by the herd. The girl continued to fume in silence for perhaps as much as a couple of miles. When he still showed no sign of swinging back toward the malpais, she reined up beside him, demanding, quietly furious, to be told what he was up to.

"Was kind of figuring," he said, "to lay hold of Teófilo—"

"And you think he went *this* way?"

"Don't you?" Kitchim asked, knowing damn well she didn't. Then, before she could answer, he threw in as though this settled it: "Since any chance I've got of bein' paid depends on stopping him, I expect you'd better take my word for it—"

"The word of a pistolero!"

Kitchim's glance flashed thin and cold. "Ever wonder how you'd fare if your friend with the patch took over Bavinuchi?"

He enjoyed the look that leaped into her face. He did not attempt to shove her nose in it, but rode off through the frightened huddle of peons to take over the lead with a saturnine grin, content to let her find her own level, deeming her too smart not to come up with the proper comparisons. Her with a stricken dad on her hands, a big hacienda whose riders she dared not put any trust in, a foreman she thought was stealing her blind.

Kitchim felt, by God, like he was king of the May.

XII

They came, two hours later, back onto the tracks
of the stolen cows, the paisanos and the girl giving
forth with gratifying sounds of astonishment.
Kitchim was too much up on his toes to show any
flavor of out-and-out patronage, but in the smile
he thew back at her there was just enough smug-
ness to darken her cheeks.

Ten minutes later he cut away from the sign,
angling north and east, wholly aware of her
frowns, pleased to know he'd got to her again. And
sure enough, after a spell of fuming in silence, she
came cantering up with her anticipated questions.

"Well," he said, dragging it out in a drawl, "it
should be pretty apparent we're moving faster than
they are. They may or may not have an eye on the
backtrail; in any event we'd be fools to engage in a
fight we might lose. They'll be a lot more careless

when they get where they're going."

She was watching him with mixed emotions, trying the fit of these thoughts on her tongue. Then, giving him a penetrating look, she said scathingly, "I'm to understand you've figured that out, too, and will get us there in time to lay a trap?"

"I'll do better than that," Kitchim grinned. "I'll recover the cows and nail Teófilo. How do you want him, plain broiled or parboiled?"

Her stormy glance appeared to find him insufferable, was probably halfway hoping he would come a cropper if only to prove him a windy braggart.

"And where do you think to do all this, hombre?"

"How's Guerras sound to you?"

Her eyes turned wide then flew out across the view, coming back to his face like dubious doves. "About as likely," she snapped, "as your ridiculous boasts!"

"Care to place a little bet?"

The walking horses moved perhaps a dozen strides while she chewed at this interspersed with stabbing glances. The confident look of him appeared to give her pause. She said at last, uneasily, "There's no railroad at Guerras . . . no way to dispose of cattle."

"So what are you afraid of?"

Her eyes, suddenly dark as bits of smoking sage, suggested her pride could not withstand the taunt. Up went her chin. "What sort of bet, hombre?"

"If this comes out the way I said, Bavinuchi's

going to need a new boss of vaqueros. I want the job."

"You *do* think big, don't you! And what happens if this fails, if you don't save the cows or catch Teófilo? Or it turns out to be someone else?" she said scornfully.

"In that event you can write your own ticket."

She looked considerably tempted. "What have you got to lose?" he scoffed. "You can't run cows without a segundo. I came onto Bavinuchi in the first place because, by your tell of it, you'd been haunting that dive in search of a gunswift."

Her eyes rolled away and came resentfully back. "A pistolero without pistol?"

"I didn't have a gun when you talked up to Marsh. It was *you* put it into my head to see Don Luis. I suppose you settled for the best you could find. An' you could hunt a long while without—"

"Spare me your boasts, gringo. You would sell a cat for a hare, I think," she declared with a continuing slanchways look. A faint flush touched his cheeks, but he kept the tough smile on his lips, and the teasing taunt of this finally jerked out of her angry nod.

"A-a-ai-hé!" she said. "While the grass is growing the horse could starve. I accept your terms. If one is not to eat the stew who minds how it be cooked?"

There was something in the way she flung out that last which left him vaguely disquieted, but in the main he was satisfied he'd come a big step forward. If he could rid himself of Teófilo now and return to Bavinuchi as boss of vaqueros he'd be in capital shape for achieving his goal.

They sighted Guerras around four and found it scarcely larger than El Federico, a collection of mud hovels, a crooked street, a general store, a leather worker's shop, a twelve-by-twelve *carcel* for the housing of overnight prisoners. The largest building of all, and directly across from the jail, Jeff observed, housed of course the business of satisfying thirsts.

From a ridgetop perhaps a thousand yards away Jeff considered the town and laid out his strategy. The peons, he decided, should remain out of sight until they saw Don Luis' daughter in front of the cantina, at which time they would approach in pairs, one from the west, one from the south, and one from the north. At the limits of the town each man was to conceal himself and be prepared to stop anyone who appeared at all anxious to take himself elsewhere.

When he was satisfied they understood and would make some attempt to carry out these instructions, Kitchim with the girl moving in from the east, jogged their tired horses toward the center of town, swinging stiffly down in front of the cantina. "Might be some risk to this," Kitchim observed, dropping the reins, "but wherever one can it generally pays to stay within the law. So we'll talk to the man."

Matching his stride as he moved toward the jail Meetah, looking doubtful, wondered if the law might not be profiting from the steal. "It's certainly possible," Kitchim nodded. "That's the risk I mentioned, and one of the reasons I don't want anyone lighting a shuck out of here. But if we bypass the law and it comes to gunplay—which it probably will, we could find ourselves between two fires, if you know what I mean. Now back my play and let me do the talking."

She said with her chin up, "We don't even know they're coming here."

"They'll be here," Jeff growled. "I've got a bet riding on it."

The jail door swung round. "Probably wettin' his whistle. Keep behind me when we go in."

No one in Guerras appeared to mind flies. It was called *The Red Horse* and its door, too, stood wide in invitation. Narrowing his eyes Kitchim slid through the opening, Meetah close on his heels, so close she banged into him when Kitchim dropped anchor. It was all that saved him, the shine-streak of steel chunking into the doorframe with the sound of a rattler.

Kitchim yelled like crazy, knocking Meetah aside and clawing for his gun as Pito—down the length of the bar where he'd been standing with another man—opened up with a pistol. But he was firing too fast, flustered by Jeff's shouts. Kitchim's first shot spun him half around; his second took the other man just above the belt. You could see the fellow cave, both hands grabbing at the front of him, the half-drawn gun dropping uselessly onto the floor, its owner folding after it. Pito, groaning, lost his grip on the bar.

It was over that quick. Jeff never did find out who had thrown the knife.

The barkeep, white-faced and shaking, had both hands above his head, eyes big as saucepans. The girl, when Jeff had chance to notice her, looked like she could use a drink. "Get some help for that feller," Kitchim growled at the apron, though it was pretty apparent the man was past earthly aid.

Kitchim went behind the bar and filled two shot glasses, downing one, handing the other to Meetah. "Throw this into you," he told her brusquely and, when she had done so, hustled her out. In the street he said, "Find me one of those boys about the size of that jasper I knocked over first—some fellow who's got something under his hat besides hair."

Without waiting to see if she were going to or not, he ducked back inside, catching hold of the bartender, hauling him round. "Which of those birds I shot is the law?"

The man's frightened stare skittered away and came back. Sweat filmed his cheeks. He rubbed a hand across his face. "*Tampoco, señor*—neither one."

"What! Where is he, then?"

"The law she ees gone to—how you say—veesit sick madre." He rubbed the flats of his hands against the soiled apron. "Three horas since—hees promo 'ave come from Porvenir."

Slick enough, Kitchim thought, seeing again in his head the beefy grin of Teófilo. Decoying the man away from town had been easier and cheaper than courting blackmail trying to buy him. "Get the clothes off that one," he growled, pointing at Pito," and went back to the street.

He found Meetah coming up with a tall, stringy peon who had a cast in one eye. She said, "This is Eduardo."

"Good man," Kitchim nodded, and pointed him toward the door of the cantina. "I want you to put on the clothes of a robber. They're waiting inside—*andale, hombre!*"

He followed him in and, while the fellow was changing, took the barkeep aside. "I don't say you're mixed into this but I guess you know what's been going on—with the cows," he said grimly.

Having no real hope of getting anything Jeff was jubilantly astonished when the fellow, devoutly establishing the Sign, while denying complicity reluctantly admitted an understanding of the situation. It tempted hope in Kitchim his luck might be taking a turn for the better and, crowding this, he said fiercely, "The young lady you just saw is of the Hacienda Bavinuchi, daughter of Don Luis. In regard for your health tell me quickly and dependably how Bavinuchi cattle have come into and departed this community in recent times." Lifting the reloaded pistol from his belt Kitchim fingered it suggestively.

The whey-faced wretch bade the Virgin strike him dead if he twisted the truth by so much as a single hair. Everyone knew, he explained, he was just a simple man who took his living from God's charity and could tell no more than he had himself heard, having set forth which he proceeded—interspersed with nervous glances at the snout of Jeff's gun—to describe the regrettable arrangements.

"And this arroyo," Kitchim pressed, "where the cows change hands before crossing the river—how do I find it?"

Armed with the information Jeff, beckoning Eduardo, returned to the street where he told the girl, "We'd best get a move on. The rendezvous is west of town a couple of miles and Teófilo's not likely to be in a very good temper if his partners in this venture aren't on hand to take delivery."

The girl's eyes widened. "You know the place?"

"Near enough," Kitchim answered, wondering about Fell who'd been told to keep an eye on Pito and that other one.

Speculation stirred behind her glance when Jeff gruffly bade her gather in the others and he'd catch up with them shortly. "Walk the horses and don't stir more dust than you have . . . Here—wait!" he growled, having caught sight of Fell propping up the front of the saddle shop yonder. "You, over there! You look the kind that can take care of himself. Want to earn a few bucks?"

Mattie Fell, pushing erect, shoved himself off the wall, narrowing stare lewdly rummaging the girl in man's pants before reluctantly swiveling his jaw toward Jeff. "You talkin' at me, mate?" He'd come into the West by way of the Horn and in unguarded moments sometimes dropped a few words he'd picked up while at sea. "Doin' what?" he said, glowering.

"Helping get back a few cows from some rustlers. Good pay in it for you and maybe a job if you turn out to be as tough as you look."

Fell's surly stare looked as rough as a cob. "An' who are you, matey?"

The girl peered more sharply at Jeff when he said, "Boss of vaqueros for the Hacienda Bavinuchi," but she kept her thoughts buried. Fell's tone was scornful: "An I'm Bucky O'Neil! Le's see the color of your dinero if there's more t' this than hogwash."

Kitchim, considerably riled, was minded to tell the son of a bitch where to go when the girl, cool as a well chain, hauled a poke from her pocket and tossed him a gold piece, arrogant as one scattering pearls before swine.

Fell's jaw dropped but he wasn't above scrounging around in the dust of the road to retrieve it. Kitchim's lip curled but he needed Fell's gun if they were to stop Teófilo and make good his boast. Those peons of Meetah's probably couldn't hit the broad side of a barn! "You have a horse, hombre?"

"Sure I got a horse."

"Get on it then and find me a rifle, and find one for yourself if you don't already have one."

"Takes dinero t' buy rifles."

"Take 'em out of that twenty if you can't get

them no other way," Jeff said and Fell, grumbling and scowling, took himself off between the ends of two buildings.

"Think he'll come back!" Meetah asked, and Jeff snorted. "With that gold in his jeans you couldn't keep him away with a carreta of switches!" And, sure enough, before they'd rounded up the rest of their outfit. Mattie Fell appeared on a flax-maned sorrel with the butts of two rifles joggling over his knees.

Kitchim, catching the weapon Fell tossed him, very nearly forgot his great need for this fellow. "This the rest of your army?" the gunman sneered, eyeing them. Kitchim, inwardly seething, hauled his eyes off the single shot Remington to growl, "Let's see the one you got," suspecting from the look of the butt it was a magazine loading U. S. Army .30 caliber. Jeff put out his hand but Fell with a grin sidled his mount out of reach. "Best I could do fer you, mister. Where-at's them rustlers you want me t'plant?"

"Man could pretty easy wear out his welcome," Kitchim said thinly. But for the moment, anyway, there wasn't much he could do about it.

Leaving Fell at the head of the column with the girl he pushed on ahead to scout out the place where—according to the barkeep—the transfer of cattle was supposed to come off.

There seemed a better than even chance the guy had lied his damned head off but when Jeff came to the barranca and cautiously quartered it from a

brush-shaded rim a child could have guessed cattle
had been driven this way more than once. The
ground was laced with the marks of their hooves
and the droppings he examined were obviously
weeks old. Climbing out he beckoned up the others
and spied a dust coming out of the wavering south
that could hardly be attributable to anything but
cattle.

There was plenty of cover along the east rim but
the opposite bank stood bare as a bridle, less pre-
cipitous too and altogether unsavory from Jeff's
turn of mind. Certainly it would prove no obstacle
to any bunch of wild critters stampeded by gunfire.

With a jerk of the chin he summoned Fell aside.
"That don't look so good," the guy muttered, following Jeff's glance. "Whoever picked this place
sure as hell wasn't figgerin' to be sucked into no
trap. By the way, who's the filly?"

Kitchim's stare turned ringy. "That's the old
man's daughter. Stay away from her, Fell."

The gun fighter's glance went over Jeff's shoulder for another brightening look. "You know me,"
he ribbed, "strictly business an' cash on the bar-
relhead."

"I won't tell you again."

Fell, brashly grinning, dug Jeff in the ribs. "In a
pardnership deal it's share an' share a—"

Jeff's whistling fist, exploding against the bones
of the man's face, took Fell out of the saddle as
though driven headlong into the jut of a limb.

He hit heavily, spraddled out, and took his time

getting up, looking meaner than fish eggs rolled in sand. Too late, staring into that ugly regard, Kitchim realized the depth if not the scope of his mistake. Still riled, breathing hard, he made no attempt to assuage the man's feelings, knowing such an effort would be taken by Fell for either weakness or fear.

Instead he said like he was talking to dirt, "Don't put your mouth to her again."

XIII

The ambush was organized with dispatch, care and all the cold-blooded purpose a man of Jeff's experience could bring to a task demanding so large a division of authority among so motley a crew. Each of them had his job and was painstakingly rehearsed for precision and savvy, not even the girl being left out of these arrangements. So few to throw against so many, the odds being feverishly against his objective when balanced in comparative quality as respecting the caliber of the two opposing teams.

He dared not count on the girl yet was forced to —the same applying to any help he might expect from Fell.

The six peons from Bavinuchi were probably loyal but ignorant, untrained and untried, not used to thinking for themselves, unskilled in the use of either arms or horses. He dismounted and scattered them in the brush of the east rim with their repeated instructions and hodgepodge of weaponry —all but the judas goat, the man picked to play the role of Pito.

This one with Meetah, who might pass in the fellow's hat for Pito's erstwhile companion, he posted beside a small hastily arranged fire built in the ashes of an older one in the barranca itself, off to one side of the hoof-gouged trail in a rubble of fallen rock. With them he placed Fell, and their trio of horses he ground-hitched nearby. To further this appearance of encampment boredom he had the girl with her hidden hair pushed up under the hat hunkered beside the fire with Eduardo—the one garbed as Pito—busied with a skillet. Fell suddenly slouched nearby on a rock, rifle concealed behind an outstretched leg. All the rest of the horses were tied back out of sight.

"The idea," Kitchim murmured, "is to fetch Teófilo and most of his helpers as close to this point as can be before I start the ball rolling." Eyeing Meetah, he said, "At the first hint of gunplay you drop flat on the ground."

Glancing again toward the dust, which seemed now scarcely more than a half mile away, Jeff picked up his single-shot Remington and stepped behind a brush-fringed boulder directly confronting the approach of the herd.

He was resigned to a stampede, knowing the cows would inevitably bolt that low and easily scaled west bank. What he hoped to prevent was the escape of the robbers; he'd instructed his companions to drop as many as possible, specifically directing Fell with his repeater to make sure of the big-bellied foreman in the event, through some fluke, Jeff failed in this himself.

With nothing to do now but wait and hope Kitchim, able from his position to keep an eye on the three by the fire, had plenty of time to regret the mad impulse that had made him tie into Fell the way he had. The man's allegiance at best had been highly problematical. There was now no telling what the fellow might do. He'd be plagued by the need to get back at Jeff—might even tell Meetah what Kitchim was up to as a means of getting even while advancing his chances to climb into Jeff's boots. He had the bone-seasoned look of this kind of a bastard. Only the man's inbred caution gave Jeff any hope at all, and it was hardly a thing a guy would want to sink or swim by.

Kitchim could not think what had set him off, why he'd reacted with such violence to the man's salacious gabble. The girl was nothing but a pawn in the high stakes game Jeff was playing. If he was minded to marry her it was not for the lure of any roll in the hay but strictly as a means of arriving more surely—more advantageously—at the goal already hung up for himself.

He could hear the hooves, the clack of horns, and peering through the yellowing fronds of salt cedar he saw the lead riders with the van of the herd lumbering into plain sight against the pall of dun dust being raised by their passage. He got

down behind his rock, sleeving the sweat from his
eyes, rubbing the palms of his hands against his
thighs. Once he'd fired its one shot this rifle was
useless. He had no reloads, which was the principal
reason for wanting this bunch to come up close
where he'd have at least a chance of maybe scoring
with his pistol.

He heard Teófilo's lusty yell sail through the
rumble of hooves; saw Eduardo straighten out of
his crouch and half turn by the fire to wave before
setting his empty skillet aside, its emptiness being
another piece of carelessness Kitchim should have
noticed and corrected, but the breeze, at least, was
luckily blowing from the herd, so maybe it
wouldn't matter that there was no smell of frying
meat in the air.

And perhaps, in itself, this wouldn't have mat-
tered. But there were other small lacks, insignifi-
cant alone but breeding in the aggregate an at-
mosphere at variance with the feel Jeff had tried to
build into this camp scene. Teofilo a hundred yards
away commenced to frown·and fan his eyes about.

The next hitch occurred when Eduardo, rising,
put the side of his face with the white eye forward
and Teófilo—now barely fifty yards from the fire—
threw up a hand to warn his outfit; and the fitful
breeze chose that moment to send Meetah's borrowed hat kiting, dumping that mane of black hair
about her shoulders.

With a snarl the boss vaquero—as Eduardo
froze—spun his horse on hind legs and Jeff, that
instant firing, missed, to frustratedly watch the

yelling Mexican, flat against his barreling mount, go streaking up that broken west bank in the van of the herd's wild bolt from flame-gouting brush and the crack-crack of rifles.

The place was a bedlam of frenzied confusion crammed with the bawling of terrified cattle and the cries and shouts of frantic men. Kitchim, dropping the Remington, grabbed up his pistol and, charging into the open, ran cursing and firing after the fleeing vaqueros, hearing the steady vicious racket of Fell's smoke-wreathed repeater.

Three spurring riders clawed the crumbling bank, made it to the top and fell back as though cut from their saddles by the swing of some monstrous unseen scythe. One riderless mount, reins flying, achieved comparative safety, only to go screaming up on hind feet and collapse in a thrashing blood-gouting fall.

It was over that sudden.

Jeff, numb in the backwash of that mad din, looked around at the huddled lumps of dead bodies. He was not one to retch, but the need churned through him, brassy as bile. Someone moved out yonder, feebly throwing up a hand. Fell's rifle cracked and the shape collapsed. More than anything else this kicked up Jeff's fury, the callous wantonness of it stirring all his frustrations.

Yet he kept his lip buttoned, the surging temper locked back of grinding teeth.

There were seven dead riders, two dead peons and three others who'd been nicked or creased but could still sit a saddle well enough to get on with it.

They were faced with the task of rounding up the cows. He saw the girl's worried look but, ignoring it, dropped back to ride with Fell when they set out through the lengthening shadows reaching down from the hills to see how many they could find.

"When we gettin' down t' cases?" Fell growled.

"Straightaway." The two governments involved, Kitchim told him, by the treaty of 1905 had agreed that all parcels of land moved by shifting channels from one side of the river to the other should be regarded, while remaining in these new positions, as land ceded by the loser to the country now possessing them—ownership, however, to remain in the hands of the original proprietors unless they refused citizenship or otherwise disposed of same.

"An' how does that help us?" Fell grumbled.

"Do you think a lone female, or a girl with a sick dad—stuck with riders she can't depend on, is fixed to put up much of a fuss against a pair of tough gringos determined to take over?"

Fell, scowling, said, "Well, but . . . Hell's fire! You don't even know there's gonna *be* a new channel—"

"There'll be one, all right. That's where you come in, but there'll be one if I have to dig it myself."

"Dig?" Fell said, and stared open-mouthed. "Y' mean I'm supposed t' dig it? Jesus Christ, man—"

"It ain't all that rough," Kitchim said with curled lip. "There's a natural valley swings. All we need's about forty foot of bed and a good charge of sticks to blow her in. Day after tomorrow I'll give

256

you a look at it. All we'll need is a storm to make
it look good and, come the next morning,
Bavinuchi'll wake up to find it's part of Texas. Put
your mind to it, feller. There we'll be, tucked in
pretty as two sixshooters riding the same belt."

Kitchim reckoned he may have over-simplified it
somewhat but in a hurried-up view this was the
plan he carried in his head, this was the long-
nourished blueprint for success on which he was
staking his life's biggest gamble. And he didn't by
God, see how it could miss. The deflection of the
river into the trough of that valley would require
nothing more than he had told Fell it would; forty
feet of twenty-foot channel and about ten sticks of
dynamite. It wasn't deflecting the channel that
worried him, it was the matter of female un-
reasonableness, the femaleness of viewing every
brought-up thing or subject as they wanted to see
it. Logic meant nothing at all to a woman and he
was far from convinced, once they'd changed the
channel, Meetah Capistrano could be made to realize she had lost Bavinuchi.

The harder he looked at this business of Meetah
the more inclined Kitchim was to re-evaluate his
hand. And he didn't have to study his cards much
to see that the best way around her was a trip in
double harness.

For a while as the hours dragged past he considered the possibilities of conversational wedlock,
of simply leading her to *think* it was the object of
his court; and with some women a deal of that kind
might have worked, the final disillusionment

257

knocking the fight all out of them.

He couldn't believe it would with Meetah. Certainly not while Teófilo was still around to be bargained with! Or Fell and his cupidity! As long as she had one fist left she'd fight!

Fiercely scowling Kitchim reckoned the surest and shortest way to Bavinuchi was to marry the ranch.

XIV

It wasn't like she was ugly, one -legged or purely given to running-off at the mouth. Or because she was Mex—he didn't care about that. He could still feel the pull of her burning all through him, making scriggly prickles flush up and down his spine. But a man liked to figure he wore the pants in his family and with a filly like Meetah you couldn't ever be more than twenty per cent sure.

They got the cows home, the big bulk of them anyhow, Teófilo powerfully conspicuous by the fact of his absence—not once had they crossed even a sign of the man. Nor was Kitchim misled into thinking he'd seen the last of the fellow. He could not be even reasonably certain the three or four hombres who had disappeared with him had not since returned to be caught up in the chores he handed out each morning as boss of vaqueros.

The first thing he'd done after being named foreman was to make a brief to-do of elevating Eduardo—the man who'd played Pito at the camp in the barranca—to the post of segundo, second in command, an innovation little relished by the rank and file of riders who, although under orders, liked to look upon themselves as considerably better than mere peons.

Kitchim, despite their dark looks, went ahead with it anyway, wanting—regardless of shortcomings—to feel he'd have one man whose loyalty he could count on. Fell he took on as hired gun, ostensibly as insurance against rustlers. "You won't have to show up every night at headquarters if it should seem inconvenient—I'll cover you there," Jeff said while they were riding out a few days later to have a look at Fell's project. "May take a week or so to get through with that digging. I'll fetch a couple peons out with tools and grub tomorrow. We're coming into the time of rain. The sooner you get the thing ready the better."

Fell, scowling, grunted. "Seems," he mentioned after mulling it over, "I'm gettin' stuck with the heavy end of this," and considered Jeff dourly. "You sure I'm down in your books fer half?"

Kitchim, catching the hard glint of Fell's probing stare, said, "I don't hardly see how I could cross you up short of bringin' this to gunplay."

"See that you remember it—I don't figger to be caught nappin'." Fell snarled in a blustery tone.

That night Jeff told Meetah, "We could do with a few dug tanks on this spread. Think I'll take a couple of your boys out tomorrow and look around. Any runoff we catch from the rains, if we could store it, would open up—"

She said, apparently uninterested in the details of ranch management, "I think you'd better send someone for that doctor again."

"Your father's worse?"

"I don't know that he's worse. He doesn't seem much better." She said broodingly, "That arm is still stiff. I can't seem to make out half he says anymore and sometimes . . . sometimes I don't think he hears me at all."

"I'll send someone straightaway," Jeff said, but she caught at his hand. "Tomorrow will do." Her eyes searched his queerly. "Have you known many women?"

What was a fellow supposed to make out of that? Kitchim peered at her uneasily. "I've known a few," he said gruffly.

"Were they prettier than I?"

"Dance-hall women most of them," Jeff growled. Then he scraped up the nerve to say, "I've never known a girl like you before," and waited, scarce breathing, to see how it hit her.

She seemed almost to stop breathing too for a moment. Then she dropped his hand and stepped back. "I must go now."

The Doc, when he came, had very little to say. Jeff wasn't around but Meetah told him later it was the medico's opinion her father's chances of recovery were hardly worth discussing, that another stroke would kill him. The girl sighed. "He's to be

kept warm, kept in bed, and to avoid excitement."
She appeared pretty gloomy.

Kitchim, sorry for her but behind this surface
sympathy jubilant at the upswing in prospects her
words seemed to herald, caught hold of her im-
pulsively. Bone deep in his own needs he said with
the words tumbling over each other, "It's too much
for a girl to be forced to shoulder . . . all this trouble over the cows, that crazy Teófilo stirring up dis-
content—in his need for revenge plotting only the
Lord knows what kind of devilment, and your
father in no shape to comfort or help. Marry me,
Meetah! Let me take care of—"

The torrent of words piled up in his throat.
Aghast he peered at the enormous eyes staring
back at him, at the shock and astonishment so na-
kedly apparent . . . the stiffening composure glaring through this incredulity as breeding and back-
ground stirred gathering flecks of scorn and indignation into the coalescing fusion of a fiercening
resentment.

Suddenly appalled at his temerity Kitchim
grabbed his hat and stumbled from the room.

During the weeks that followed while the ditch
was being dug, Kitchim, up to his ears in the thousand and one details of managing a ranch of
Bavinuchi's magnitude, saw little of the girl, discovering no chance of talking with her alone.
Teófilo had disappeared as though the very bowels
of the earth had opened up to swallow him.

Jeff, keeping in touch with what transpired in the

house through conversations conducted with the servants by Eduardo, learned of Don Luis' continuing decline. The master of Bavinuchi on a diet of broths no longer concerned himself with matters of this planet, the segundo reported. Shrunken beyond belief, Jeff was told, the old man lay in a kind of trance, perhaps communicating with God.

"He is not long for this world," Eduardo said, piously crossing himself to ward off bad luck. "The señorita? A-a-ai-hé! She is sad and pale like a wilted flower. She sits all the time by the bed watching, I think, for el hombre of the Black Horse."

It was hard for Jeff to picture her so. She had seemed so alive, so crammed with life's juices. He cursed himself for a bungling fool. If he'd been content to let well enough alone . . . Well, no matter, he thought, anxiously scanning the skies, his original plan was as good now as ever. Fell's ditch was almost ready. Thrown back on his former intention he found it difficult to see—surrounded as she was by the hacienda's isolations—what the heir to Bavinuchi could do to circumvent him. He could keep her a prisoner indefinitely if he had to.

The mayordomo? Kitchim's lips twisted. Another doddering ancient with his snags of bad teeth and silly half senile chuckles. He had nothing to fear from a man who spent most of his few wakeful hours waylaying opportunities for pinching girls' bottoms. The reins of government were in Kitchim's hands.

It would have to rain sometime. One good storm

plus those little yellow sticks would lift the river from its channel.

But he didn't know about the fat-bellied man keeping tab on Fell's progress from the cover of the hills. . . .

In the shank of an afternoon three days later the first fat drops fell out of wind-tossed clouds to lance the smoky film of heat and thwack against the drought-parched earth with the spattering force of liquid hail. The peons looked up with gleeful grins, riders went phlegmatically about their chores and half an hour later the sun broke through, much to Kitchim's disgust.

Two thunder showers, six hours apart, raced across the thirsty earth the next day, neither of them robust enough to develop any lengthy stands of water. Fell rode in about dark grinning hugely. "Must've had a real gully washer north of here someplace. River's up three foot an' still risin'. There's a soft spot in that stretch we left. Ditch is ready—why not blow her tonight?"

Kitchim eyed him tight-lipped. "Keep your voice down, you fool! You want to tell the whole country?"

"Hell, these peons—"

"The crew just rode in. They're already curious—"

"An' small wonder," Fell flared, "the way you've had 'em shiftin' cattle ag'in' the river this last week—I been some curious myself. What you tryin' t' do—put 'em *all* on this banco?"

Jeff had told him not to use that word around

headquarters and this aggravation, topping the suspicion in the man's tone and eyes, made it hard to keep his hands off the fellow. Grinding down on his rage he growled, "Don't bother unsaddling. We're going back out there."

A hot wind blew the length of the valley. Fell against orders had come in that way and was aware that Jeff knew this. With his hat pushed back the rusty red of his hair matched the jerky brightness looking out of that too narrow, too foxy, slanch of eyes.

He was like a spring wound too tight, and the look of him warned Kitchim the tiger-faced Texan had more on his mind than that disreputable hat. He could feel the excitement churning back of Fell's stare, as now the man said, "We ain't goin' t' need fifty riders once we cut this chunk off from the rest of it. All the shots are in place. It's goin' t' storm again t'night, so how's about takin' half the crew along with us?"

"I don't quite catch the drift of it," Jeff said.

"A lot of them fellers ain't goin' t' be too happy when they find this spread's become a part of Texas. Time t' get shut of 'em's right now before we blow it. An' we ain't got much time—river's eatin' into that bank right now."

"Guess I'm too pooped to cope with riddles, Matt. Just say right out what you've got in mind."

"Look," Fell said. "Be a deal of confusion—bound t' be. Right? We don't want anyone draggin' their feet, that's fer sure. Some of these hombres is goin' t' resent you bein' put over 'em—hell, a lot of these Mexicans got no use fer Americans. My idee, once we've blown in this banco, is keep the girl under wraps until she signs the spread over, an' we don't want around a lot of yaps that'd take up f' her. *I* say git rid of 'em before they git their backs up or open their mouths."

"And how do we do this?"

"Show 'em that cut. Git 'em pokin' round in it and then blow the whole works."

Kitchim's stomach turned over. Yet he wasn't— not really—too terribly astonished. To the gun fighter's conscienceless warped way of thinking this cold-blooded proposal offered a logical solution to the control of Bavinuchi. And he was obviously pleased with himself for having hit on it. What occupied Jeff was the way this spelled out the big difference between them . . . and the uncomfortable picture the man's words set up of how far down the no-return trail he'd come himself. There was no essential difference between what Fell had in mind for Meetah and the way Jeff had figured on handling her.

Forgotten was the river and self interest as Kitchim, like a man shaken out of a dream, looked around and saw himself as he most probably looked to others. He didn't like what he saw and shook his head as though to change it, hearing the gun fighter stir and clear his throat with some impatience.

The fishbelly shine of those grinning eyes reminded Jeff that Fell was waiting for some ex-

pression of approval. What could he say to him—
what *dared* he say?

To give himself time to iron out his own thinking
he said, "Maybe I will take a few of them out there.
Not too many. When we move this deal into Texas
we want a strong enough crew to make sure we
hang onto it. Wait here. I'll see what I can come up
with."

He strode off into the dark, the feel of the man's
eyes stabbing into his back like the jab of steel
needles.

He was too torn with doubts to think clearly,
running into blank walls every way he turned. It
wasn't just Fell or that greedy Texas marshal that
bothered him half as much as did the pictures he
kept seeing of that goddam girl.

Turning into the lamplit mess shack his glance
quartered over the hands who'd come in, primari-
ly looking for men he believed would stick with the
ranch if anything came up which might tend to test
loyalties. He reckoned four would be enough to
handle the vague and still tentative notion that
kept sliding around through the churn of his
thoughts, and gave his selections the nod as he
made them. The four followed him out.

In the starlight he said, "We're ridin'. It could be
a rough trip so pick the best, freshest mounts you
can put your ropes on."

He could feel their curiosity as they moved toward the pens. They asked no questions. When
they'd caught their mounts, the saddling completed

267

they looked to him for orders. Kitchim growled at
them gruffly, "You may see some queer things
where we're fixin' to go. You are not under orders.
You will do what you think—each in his own heart
—is best for Bavinuchi. Without regard for anything else. Is—"

A sound no louder than the snapping of a stick
jerked Jeff's chin toward the windows of the house.
Only one of these showed light, and most of this
was filtered through a screen of bougainvillea.
"Stay put!" Kitchim grunted, and broke into a
run, knowing that sound for the report of a shot.

The guard had come out of his box at the gate to
peer open-mouthed toward that one spot of light.
Kitchim, rattling the grill, thought the fool would
never turn. "*Let me through!*" he snarled, and was
bitterly afraid, mind leaping ahead with its visions
of Teófilo as he tore through the tangle of foliage
that separated him from the portal.

The door was open, and the door beyond. Over
the heads of a goggling huddle of servants, gun still
in hand, he could see Mattie Fell with his wolflike
grin closing in on the girl. He had her backed into
an angle of the patio wall. The knife in her hand
was all that kept Fell from grabbing her.

To take the girl out of line Jeff was forced to
move in from the side. He dared not take his eyes
from the man. Yet so engrossed was Fell it wasn't
until Jeff thumbed back the hammer of his pistol
that the gun fighter suddenly awoke to his peril.

He spun like a cat, eyes slitted, gun lifting in a
burst of livid flame. One of those slugs flung

Kitchim half around. Then his own gun spoke. Fell's eyes went wide and you could see shock travel all through his face, and like that he stood perhaps another half minute. With a terrible effort he tried to bring up his gun. His legs let go and he pitched suddenly forward, dead before he struck. Only then did Kitchim notice Don Luis' crumpled shape with the blood pooling round it.

The girl, he saw, was on the verge of hysteria. He caught hold of her, shook her. "It's time you learned," he growled, "life's no bowl of goddam roses!" and slapped her stingingly across both cheeks. She tried to use the knife she still held and he cuffed it, clattering, into the fountain. Nodding, he said, "That's better—come on!"

She was like a child in his grip, her resistance ridiculous. When she saw how useless it was she quit struggling and presently, breathless, found herself at the gate.

The guard let them through. A look at Jeff's face left the questions piled up behind his scared stare. Meetah, hustled along in Kitchim's fiercening grip, arrived at the corrals and saw the shadowy shapes of waiting men. "She goes with us," Kitchim said. "José, give the lady your horse—you stay here."

In the saddle Meetah said, "Where are you taking me?"

"Perhaps to see the end of a world."

Tearing through the black night with its drizzle of rain he didn't know himself what he might finally do. All his values were unsettled and the notions now haring around in their place he couldn't understand. It seemed crazy to throw away all he had worked for . . . he didn't know if he could do it.

He spoke abruptly to the girl. "Do you know what a banco is?"

She shook her head—he could see that much. "You stand a damn good chance of bein' on one before morning." Gruffly then he told her of the treaty between the United States and Mexico whereby one stood to lose what the other gained as a result of the Rio Grande changing its bed. "Would you swear allegiance to the gringo flag?"

"I would have to think about it. Why is this important?"

"The river's up. The west bank, where we're going, looks in danger of being undercut. A lot of that rock has turned out to be rotten. Fell's had two of your paisanos working there, making a ditch."

The girl, saying nothing, continued to watch him as the horses took them into heavier rain. "A ditch," Kitchim growled, "that'll bring the Rio rolling down this trough an' practically into Bavinuchi's back yard."

Soaked to the skin they huddled in the leathers while the floundering horses carried them north and east and the rain drummed into the slickening earth. She was silent so long Jeff reckoned she hadn't heard or couldn't make out the significance of what he'd said.

She'd understood right enough, had probably caught every word. The trust in her reply while she peered through the dark was like a knife turning in him, its bite slicing deeper than the slug from Fell's gun. She said, "You'll know how it happened. You can tell them the truth."

Lightning skipped along the rim of the world, distant thunder rolled through the rain and the ground was a sea of glistening mud. The horses, floundering now, seemed to spend half their strength trying to keep legs under them and you could feel the strain in their trembling flanks.

The cold of the night got into Jeff's bones. A gust of wind slammed against them and the slog of the rain was like a pounding from fists, beating Jeff into the trap of his thoughts. *Bavinuchi!* he snarled, and it was like a curse, as though he were beginning to wish he'd never heard of the place.

Some might think this a pretty barren region to be getting so worked up about, but never a man who knew the West. Desolate, remote, uncultured and uncared for—it was all of these, and vast and still, crammed with dangers and steeped in violence, too hot and too bright with its barbaric vistas and sand-scoured heights, its fierce winds and cruel droughts, flash floods and storms that could boil out of nowhere and in a matter of minutes wipe away a life's work. It was cattle land, cow country, good for man and good for beast. Even cut in half by the river—as Kitchim planned—the hacienda could be made to support every critter he'd gathered, including horses. Too much to give up for a crazy whim! For a girl who thought him no better than dirt!

She could never hang onto it—no woman could.

There was more lightning now, great sizzling bolts of it ripping open the skies, the heavy tumble of thunder seeming almost incessant. It was hard to guess how far they had come but they must, Kitchim reckoned, be getting close to that ditch. And then, in an unconscionably bright, all-encompassing flash the whole world seemed to explode. Shocked and gasping they pulled up, numbly staring at each other. "Was that thunder?" Meetah cried in a jumpety voice.

Through the drumming of rain a new sound swelled like wind ballooning into a monstrous roar. In a lurid flash Kitchim saw it—a solid twenty-foot wall of churning water rushing toward them out of the rain-lashed night.

"The river! Kitchim shouted, swinging his rein-ends at the rump of Meetah's terrified horse. "Out of here—*out!*" he yelled, spurring frantically after her.

The horses needed no urging. Ears flattened, eyes rolling, they lunged from the trough. Slipping, sliding, twisting and squealing in the suck of that muck, they floundered, spent and wheezing, onto high ground.

"There's no good—" Jeff began, and let the words fall away as he followed, with rain-blurred stare, the rigid stretch of a vaquero's arm.

Three riders, head on, were pounding out of the storm, a dark huddle of shapes in the slant of the rain until a jagged lemon flash limned them stark for what they were. The burly shoulders of the man in the middle—the lead rider—grabbed all of Jeff's attention. The streaming patch and flash of teeth behind the bristle of ragged mustachios brought a shout of "Teófilo!" churning up out of him as he clawed for his gun.

The jump of the butt kicking hard at his palm was a beautiful feeling—but a greater satisfaction boiled through his veins when he saw the renegade reel in his saddle and with outflung arms go ass-over-elbows off the back of his mount.

They were all firing now and, that quick, it was finished.

In the receding rumble of departing thunder the sound of the river was a grinding roar, filling their minds with its tumult and import. Kitchim's banco now was an established fact, but there was no triumph in him, just the bitter taste of a despair he could not fathom.

Perhaps, in part, the loss of blood from the bite of Fell's slug had something to do with this wrung-out feeling; he hardly seemed his usual self, but a bullet creased biceps wasn't serious enough to fill his head with the kind of damned bilge he was finding there.

He looked around through the slackening thinness of rain and disgustedly blew some of the drip off his nose. "We might as well go back."

No one raised any objections.

Kitchim found himself someway paired off with the girl and it was Meetah who presently broke the morose silence he seemed to have built around him. "I had never dreamed to find Bavinuchi a part of Texas."

He said nothing to that.

But she was not discouraged. Stars were beginning to liven up the black and as the trail took them farther from the sound of the river and the grunting racket of gleeful frogs, still eyeing him she said in a thoughtful tone of voice, "You weren't planning to quit, were you?"

"I'd probably better," he grumbled. "You don't need me—"

"But without you to show me, how would I ever keep the rest of those Texans from stealing Bavinuchi?"

The old pull was still there. Kitchim scowled at her irritably. "It wasn't Fell that was planning to steal it—it was *me*," he said bluntly.

"How very enterprising of you. And how did you think to ever get title, or hadn't you gotten that far?" she asked coolly.

"I was going to shut you up somewhere till you signed the place over."

She put her head on one side. "I could fall in love with a man that resourceful."

"A gringo?" Kitchim said, staring.

The gamin grin crossed her lips. "You might stay around and find out," she suggested.

Sure-Fire Entertainment From Ace Westerns

Nelson Nye

Winners of the SPUR and WESTERN HERITAGE AWARD

Sharp Shooting and Rugged Adventure from America's Favorite Western Writers